BLOODY FOOTPRINTS AROUND THE CAMPFIRE

DECLAN BURNETT

SEVERED PRESS
HOBART TASMANIA

BLOODY FOOTPRINTS AROUND THE CAMPFIRE

CHAPTER ONE
SISSY WHITE

Being alone didn't always mean lonely. Sissy White watched out the window of the Greyhound as it rolled southbound through the green, green forests of Washington. It looked just like home to her and that was far from easing. Home could be a scary place; home was where she'd nearly died a horrible, violent death.

Close to home, in those seemingly identical forests, she'd lost the two best friends she'd ever known. Her only real friends. Since, she hadn't been able to open up emotionally. So, in her case, alone did indeed mean lonely.

And she'd seen them die. Smelled it and heard it, and almost died, too. But she'd survived, and she'd tried to move on. The news and all the people online, most ranged from insinuating that she was a liar to downright accusing her of lying. The police were better, she figured this was because they saw the scene, witnessed the carnage first-hand. No way did her 5'2" and 159 pounds tear a full-grown man and his large girlfriend to shreds. Not going to jail, not even being a suspect, these facts didn't let her move on from what had happened. In fact, the violence was now shackled to her ankle like a leg iron.

Now here she was, jumping headfirst back into the scene she'd desperately tried to leave behind. "Money's money," she said, her forehead leaned against the cool glass of her window.

The bus was more than halfway empty, which had been a bit of a blessing, or at least a relief. If she bumped into twenty people between twenty- and forty-years-old in the Pacific Northwest, at least one recognized her from the beastly infamy of being the survivor of a massacre. So far, on this trip, two people had recognized her. One was a thirty-something woman who'd squinted at her a few seconds before going wide-eyed, placing Sissy's face to the story. The second was a young man with a thin neck beard and a field of pimples pebbling his forehead.

"You're Sissy White!" he shouted, running up to her as she waited for the bus's door to open. "You got away with murder!"

Others began looking and she lifted her shoulders while scrunching her neck, trying to hide in the folds of her sweater. "Leave me alone," she said.

"You wish. Bitch like you, you deserve no privacy. Murderer!"

"They were my friends."

"Murderer!"

Sissy's eyes sprang tears. Since the attack, she'd been an emotional wreck. If it wasn't for needing money, she'd have stayed in her tiny apartment all day every day, live out her life in peaceful seclusion.

But she needed money and that's why she was out here. That's how this asshole got his moment to accost her.

"You should be in prison! Everybody!" The man turned, waving like he wanted an invisible DJ to pump up the crowd. All the passengers awaiting their various busses watched in quiet interest. "This bitch murdered—hey!"

A security guard in navy blue from head to ankles grabbed the man, lifting him slightly, hand firm in his armpit, and walking him away. "Let's find your bus."

"No, but, it's Sissy White! That murdering bitch!" the young man said, livid, his cheeks blotchy red.

"Whoever she is, she paid to ride a bus in peace," the security guard said and deposited the angry young man at the far end of the platform. When the security guard came back, Sissy quietly thanked him and he replied, "If you're really her, you are a murdering bitch."

Everyone hated her. Everyone but the weirdos holding the weekend-long conference at a ski lodge in the middle of summer. These people had paid her to show up and tell her story. That part would hurt, of that she had zero doubts, but it would also be okay. She'd told her story from start to finish once, and nobody believed it. She'd gotten partway through it another two dozen times, only to be stopped and asked why would she lie? Didn't she want to clear her murderous conscious? At least these people would believe her.

Though getting paid was the biggest part, and by more than a little.

She'd negotiated $15,000 for her appearance, her

story, and for all the autographs necessary. She was a perk on a ticket stub, a survivor with a tantalizing tale…she'd be that for the kind of dough they were offering.

Suddenly, the trees out the window disappeared and a fancy-looking tourist town came into view. Cabins and cottages and store after store closed for the season. The bus slowed and not far ahead was a Shell gas station. The brakes squeaked and the bus rocked on its shocks as it pulled to the curb. Once it stopped, the driver called out, "Chamberlain! Should be one of ya!"

Sissy pushed to her feet and shouldered a backpack.

"Got any luggage?" the driver said, eyeing Sissy in the mirror.

"Yes," Sissy said.

The driver made an annoyed face before she pushed to her feet. "Of course you do." She stepped out ahead of Sissy with the keys in her hand. "What's it look like?"

"It went into the second one. Just a purple and black Samsonite," Sissy said.

The lot was mostly empty, but one vehicle was parked front and center, next to a huge Monster Energy sign affixed to a yard light pole. Sitting on the hood of a beat-up Land Rover was a middle-aged man with a long red beard. He had a sign on his lap that read: S WHITE.

The driver found the bag and Sissy rolled it toward the bearded man on the hood of the SUV. "I'm Sissy White," she said, low enough that no prying ears might hear.

"Don't I know it. A real pleasure to meet you. I'm John Nolan."

To Sissy's surprised relief, he didn't hold out a hand for a shake. Instead, he pointed to her luggage. She relented her grip and he hefted, doing three quick lifts as if to weigh it.

"Feels like three days' worth of clothes." He laughed after this and swung open the door behind the driver's seat. The bag disappeared. "Well, hop in. It's only a few minutes from here."

Sissy nodded, really unsure of how to feel. This kind of immediate acceptance? If she'd ever had it, it hadn't been hers for a long, long time.

The Land Rover was loud and the stereo was on low. John turned it up, something by The Doors. "Before my time, but I love old rock. How about you?"

Sissy had to smile. She did love old rock. "Same," she said.

"Right on."

John rolled them back the way she'd come until they reached the first corner leading down a skinny asphalt road. The trees were once again thick and the grey asphalt cut through the greenery, heading up and up and up until reaching a parking lot. There was a big wooden sign that read: CHAMBERLAIN MOUNTAIN RESORT. Driven into the grass like a political advertisement next to it was another sign, one that read in big letters: SQUATCHER-CON 2022, and beneath it in much smaller lettering: WITH SPECIAL GUEST SISSY WHITE.

CHAPTER TWO
SISSY WHITE

Sissy took a tall bottle of Bacardi from her luggage, twisted free the cap, and took a small swig. It burned. It made her wince. She was forced to take a second before she chased the pair of hot, hot swigs with a third. The red digits on the alarm clock read 6:59. She was supposed to be outside for the pre-con meet and greet with the other supposed celebrities. Suddenly, she was intensely nervous and anxious. They'd paid her and she needed that money, so what choice did she have? But this was going to suck.

Another mouthful went down the hatch.

The seconds mounted and the warmth in her throat rose to her cheeks and a thin fog settled upon her brain. She considered bringing the bottle with her. It would be a long weekend without a hangover; with a hangover, the weekend would stretch for eons, would ultimately be unbearable.

The bottle went to the dresser, next to the big black TV. She scooped up her keycard. From the open closet, she took the sweater she'd slipped into before leaving home this morning and left her room.

The establishment had a roomy and well-done interior. On top of that, it had scads of finished space outside according to the map—paths that headed off in a variety of directions, decorative rocks and trees, chainsaw woodcarvings, a distant pond—it would be easy to get lost. However, the campfire was easy to find thanks to the light cast by the flames. The bright reds and oranges danced through the glass of the rear lobby windows. Even from thirty feet away, she could make out at least six figures. She inhaled a deep breath, straightened her shoulders, and pushed onward.

"There she is!" John shouted. "Our guest of honor."

There were indeed six people settled in on fine wicker furniture around a small campfire. What was a surprise was that the space hadn't been modernized. The campfire had been inset into dirt and had a ring of rocks surrounding it. Nothing fine or finished, no polish. Dirt, rocks, grass, and fire, pretty much like every campfire she'd had or been invited to...including the one that made her infamous.

"Hi," Sissy said, trying to appear casual.

"Here, here," John said, rising from his seat and pulling a white wicker chair closer to the fire.

"Thanks," Sissy said.

"Beer?" John said. "Pop? Water?"

"I guess one beer won't hurt," Sissy said.

"Thatta girl," said a woman with curly brown hair from across the fire.

Counting Sissy there were three women. She'd

kind of assumed she might be one of about two through the entire weekend, so this was a subtle nicety she'd try not to take for granted.

"Since this is your first time, and you're the big fish here, I'll give a little rundown of how these work. Perhaps it's a touch insensitive, but we have a little fun with the Alcoholics Anonymous system. In turn, we each stand and tell our personal sasquatch story, or if we've been here year after year, a good story we've gotten firsthand," John said, a big smile coming through on his words.

"Right, okay." Sissy knew this was coming, was part of the contract she'd signed. It was a nice touch that it was so intimate a group…maybe. It was also possible all these people were freaks.

She took her seat and accepted the beer: a Heineken, which was another nice surprise.

"I believe you, Freddy, started last year," John said, nodding toward a man with puffy hair and big, big sideburns.

"Yeppers," Freddy Talbott said.

Sissy tilted her head some. He seemed dejected, and she wondered if he was somehow infamous too, and had to be here.

"I have a new one, but someone else can take the lead car this year," Freddy said.

"Ooh, perfect," John said. "Do we have any volunteers?"

"Suppose I've always gone in the middle, and this year, I have my own encounter to divulge," said a pudgy man in a khaki vest with a red flannel shirt beneath, his hair thin on top while thick on the sides. He had huge, wire-rimmed glasses. The kind serial killers tended to prefer.

"Right on, Billy! You've never let us down," John said. "He's been coming since day one."

Billy Ross nodded, looking straight at Sissy while she looked at the thin hair atop his head and sipped her beer.

"Anyone have to pee before I start?" Billy said.

Everyone, including Sissy, shook their heads, though she might have to, very soon. About three ounces of rum and a can of beer was a recipe that ran right through her.

Billy cleared his throat and began.

CHAPTER THREE
BILLY ROSS

Billy pulled out of Verrill's Gas 'n Gulp and hooked a right down the long stretch of blacktop that parted what seemed like endless trees. He was more than a hundred miles from home and his eyes had already started to play games with him. He saw deer everywhere from his peripherals, and knew it was a trick the brain played to keep a man safe, to warn him to rest before it was too late.

He lowered his window and turned up the volume on the stereo. Britney Spears was demanding *Hit Me Baby One More Time*, and he tapped along. He was a high school senior when that song came out and it was enormous. So big all the girls in his class made up awful stories about Britney Spears, that she had to get semen pumped from her stomach because she sucked off so many record executives, and that she had to get her vagina reconstructed from sex with everything from vegetables to horses. They were simply jealous of the attention she got, and that all the hard rockers and metalheads and rap boys suddenly had CDs with this blonde popstar in their bags. What made it worse, she was just about their age.

He understood the jealousy of other people's attention. His classmates only ever looked at him—chubby, pimply, common, unfunny, and lower middle-income—when they wanted someone to push around. Meaning only guys looked at him. He didn't even end up going to his prom.

And now at forty, the only intimacy he'd known with women was the kind he had to pay for. Thankfully, finding a woman and experiencing physical contact had become a lot less important to him these last six or seven lonely years. Part of that was getting older, sure, but a bigger part was letting his obsession take hold of his life. No more mooning over pretty faces and curves, now it was all found hairs and footprint casts lifted from the floors of dense forests.

"*Hit me baby one mo*—" A yawn interrupted his singing and he blinked, leaning so the wind rushing through the window battered his forehead.

A sign for a state park came into view of his headlights and he decided he'd rather wrestle with his tent in the dark than die in a ditch. He pulled into the closed park and killed his engine in the big gravel lot. It was almost empty—three windshields banked the yellow glow of the yard lights—and he guessed nobody would even notice if he hopped a fence somewhere and found a clearing in the bush. He didn't like pitching his tent on private property, an old farmer had shot at him once. So, when possible, he hit up parks. Also, when possible, he snuck in without paying.

Billy had his oversized sleeping bag and pillow. The bag zipped up like a moth cocoon, right over his head, but he usually left it so he could watch the night around him, while still covering his nose. It seemed to him that an inordinate amount of heat departed the human body via the nose.

Beyond the outhouses was a rocky outcropping that then fell into a clearing. He climbed up onto the giant limestone ridge and looked at the mossy ground beneath the thin trees on the far side. A good spot for the night, surely. He climbed over and sat down to remove his boots, Britney still in his head. He slipped out of his socks before opening the strained button of his jeans and shimmied into the sleeping bag. He gave his cellphone a final glance—the time read 11:21 PM—and then zipped up to his eyes. The bag curled over his forehead and the only skin showing could've been covered by a set of aviator sunglasses.

Overhead, the moon was partially hidden behind clouds and only the nearest and brightest stars were visible. He closed his eyes and within a minute, was asleep.

His nose had slipped free of his sleeping bag and was cold, damp, runny as a dog's nose. He blinked at the black night sky.

Clunk.

He looked to his left. The rock wall. It took him a moment to understand where he was.

Clunk.

A single spark flared from the tossed rock that had hit the stone wall and was now rolling through the moss toward him.

Clunk.

No spark this time, but the rock was clearly visible, like Casper the Friendly Ghost: dead but zooming through his family's dark mansion. Billy understood then and jerked to his right. He squinted against the night and watched for another white orb.

It rose and he zoned his attention to where he assumed was an arm. Up from that assumed arm to a shoulder. From that assumed shoulder to a neck, head, face...eyes. The moon was still hidden, though not all the way.

Clunk.

Billy kept his gaze affixed on the gentle shine banking the moonlight. Sasquatches were similar to moose; there was no eyeshine when banking automobile light or flashlights or any other manmade device, but when it came from far, far overhead, light banked from the moisture.

In an instant, those eyes disappeared. Billy remained staring into the woods, at that very spot. Morning came and he rose, barefoot, and stepped to the spot of his focus. Full and big and perfect, the indent in the mossy ground was all he'd dare ask for. For lack of a better option, he unzipped his fly and let his pants fall. A place marker.

He rescued his keys from a pocket and turned away. In stressed to translucent Fruit of the Loom tighty-whities, Billy climbed over the limestone wall and ran to his car. A ranger called to him from across the parking lot. He ignored the voice. The Tupperware bin was ready as it always was.

By the outhouses, he used a water faucet and filled a plastic measuring container from within the

Tupperware bin. The ranger was behind him, only ten feet away, and shouting. Billy glanced back, offered a forced smile, and continued on. He climbed over the rock wall and there, the ranger paused, watching with his hand on his service pistol, though without taking it from its holster.

Billy was too excited about his find and what he'd experienced in the night to worry that the weapon might come free.

CHAPTER FOUR
SISSY WHITE

"He didn't bother the entire time the mold set. He didn't say much of anything, though he had that look, you know, like he was a bit excited, too. When I got to the rock wall, he asked me to pour a second cast, so he could show his kids," Billy said. He dragged a heavy carton from beside his chair to his feet. "He said he'd had all kinds of things happening not far from the campsites lately. The usual stuff: tossed rocks, partial footprints, missing fruit from coolers and strung up in trees. Then he also said it had changed some over the last handful of years. There'd been destroyed dogs and two missing campers, one time he said a little girl found a femur in a huge pile of feces."

Sissy squirmed at having to pee. She'd been made a touch upset by this story. Why hadn't this sasquatch killed him like it had her friends? Why did he get to go on living, if you could call what he did living...*though, who am I to talk?*

Billy passed a plaster cast to his right and a vial of several coarse black hairs, each as thick as the strands in a wire brush. He tossed a rock the size of a softball gently up and caught it when it came down.

"Need to powder my nose. Ladies, care to join me?" one woman said.

Without hesitation, Sissy rose, as did the other two women. The men went immediately silent, as if they'd been caught in the middle of some hot gossip they ought to know better than to spill. The other women walked with a locational confidence that suggested this wasn't their first time at the resort, or possibly that they'd simply gotten there much earlier than Sissy had. She trailed silently into the bright, bright washroom just past the lobby.

It reminded her of finally convincing her parents to send her to the same camp where her best friend Lyla spent a month every summer from grade four to grade eight. Lyla was a vet and showed Sissy where to go and what to do, who was cool and who was lame, and even convinced counselors to switch up the paperwork last second before the campers were assigned their spots. Lyla had only winked at Sissy when they announced that Sissy and Lyla were in the same bunkhouse and activity group.

But these women weren't Lyla and Lyla was gone.

Sissy took the first empty stall while the shorter and more average looking of the two took the last stall, leaving two empty stalls between. The other woman, pretty, and somewhat familiar looking stared into the mirror.

The woman down from Sissy started pissing and then let two huge farts rip. She began laughing and said, "Pardon et moi."

"You stinky bish," the woman at the mirror said, a smile on her words.

"Hey, new girl, you're that survivor, right?" the woman in the stall said.

"Yes," Sissy said, finding that despite needing to go, she also needed to push to get the party started. She fiddled with the loose threads sprouting free at the waist of her jeans. "I guess I am."

"Wild. I heard all about that, didn't buy it. But now that I see you, I kind of doubt you killed them, which only leaves your story, so I guess I'll buy it," the one from the mirrors said.

"Uh, thanks," Sissy said.

"Don't mind Amy, she's an actress. My name's Nancy, by the way," the one from the stall said.

"Actor, actress is sexist," Amy Snell said.

It took Sissy a moment, but then she got it. "You're from *Robogator*."

Nancy laughed.

"Among other things. I'm here because of my involvement in the *Bloody Footprints* series. All these stories about sasquatch slaughters, usually need a sexy girl to show her tits. They pay pretty well, better than waiting tables. These cons pay almost as well as B-horror flicks," Amy said.

"And I'm here because the universe hates my movies," Nancy Hargenson said.

"Oh?" Sissy was finished and pulled three tissue tickets free from the dispenser.

"Back when I was trying to fund this movie I wrote called *Season of Hate*, I needed money and had connections in the business. This other, not-quite-

Hollywood company offered me a quick twenty grand if I could write and film four pornos," Nancy said.

Sissy stopped, her pants up and her hand hovering an inch above the flush handle. "Pornos?"

"Yeah, she used the set from this movie called *Rise of the Yeti* and made four pretty decent porno flicks," Amy said, no sarcasm in her voice.

"Thanks," Nancy said and flushed.

"I mean it. It's almost like you weren't familiar with how stupid those movies usually are," Amy said.

Sissy flushed and stepped out.

"I was, just not recent ones. When I was a kid, my dad had a ton of movies: *Sex World, Behind the Green Door, Aunt Peg*. They had a story, sort of, at least they tried to be interesting," Nancy said.

"None of them had hot babes getting pounded by dudes in sasquatch suits," Amy said.

Sissy couldn't help but laugh as she washed her hands.

Nancy came out of her stall buttoning her jeans. "I guess for a sex movie it's weird, for a movie-movie, it's less so. It's a funny situation. The *Beastly Urges* series just kind of worked out."

"So they invite you over these movies?" Sissy said. "When did you make them?"

"Almost twenty years ago, now. It's a cult thing. I come every third year. I own the rights for those movies now, something I hadn't even considered when I signed the production company's contract," Nancy said. "I bring a few boxes of DVDs. In the past I've brought along one of the girls, but last time they'd proven to have gotten too old for the crowd in a strange way."

"Strange how?" Sissy said, leading the women out of the washroom.

Amy huffed. "These guys don't mind women getting old—crazy, right?—but they do get a bit iffy if someone gets old and has loads of mediocre plastic surgery," Amy said. "I don't get many offers to lead monster movies these days because I'm too old, but so long as I keep the collagen minimal, I can go to cons all over America. Easy money if you can stomach smelling every shade of middle-aged dude who has spent days walking around a stuffy, too warm convention hall."

Sissy had never thought about actors in that sense, nor movie makers. She pushed back out toward the patio, which led to the campfire site. The men all had their heads turned, watching for the women.

"Great, you've returned," John said. "I'm thinking to liven things up, we'll hear from Sydney next. He says he has something special for us."

Sydney Fromm straightened in his chair. He was frumpy, had a day or two's worth of beard stubble, and wore a jean jacket. "Special...I certainly hope so."

Sissy got it then, why his voice sounded familiar. "You're the writer. I recognize your voice from the *Milk of Our Soil* audiobook."

"Ha!" Sydney said. "You're one of about a hundred who caught that one. Hope you liked it."

Sissy hadn't liked it, so she just smiled.

"Anyway, the something special is a brand new short, something I came up with for just this occasion. Since I've told my mostly uneventful sasquatch story before, I figured I'd come with something new and exciting for you."

"I can't wait," John said.

The others grumbled quietly in polite agreement as Sydney withdrew his cellphone from his pocket, and began his spooky story with the light from the screen banking against his chin in a very campfire tale kind of way.

CHAPTER FIVE
SYDNEY FROMM

Jordan put gentle fingers to his head, wincing, eyes closed tight at the pain. He brought one hand away. Wet to the touch. He looked at the blood and sighed: equal parts annoyance and worry. Outside the foggy bus window was a world of snow, snow, and more snow. He glanced to the moon: a few days from full. The sigh became a groan when reality started oozing back to him.

"You all right?" a young woman asked from across the aisle. She was pale and had a black parka pulled over her arms like a muff; wore a black velvet shirt that zipped into a turtleneck and a gold necklace with a ruby—based on the gem's size, the distinction suggested that *amulet* might be the proper term and that this stone absolutely had to be a fake. Even with a colorless pallor, she was beautiful. Her hair had the right amount of hairspray and her lips had the right amount of crimson. "You hear me?" she said then when Jordan got lost in reverie—he'd cast more than a few glances her way in the preceding hours, wishing this woman would talk to him.

"I'm okay. You okay?" he said, his breath steamy on the blueish black night.

She pointed to the front of the bus. "Better than them."

Jordan looked and saw the carnage, the blood, the proof undeniable that they were up that proverbial brown river without a paddle. The bus had been hustling along above the speed limit, even in that weather, and was about midway between Fort McMurray and Edmonton on Highway 63, meaning they were hundreds of miles from anything remotely civilized. Jordan turned in his seat, thankful to locate five other survivors: two big men in bulky Carhartt jackets, two smaller men in well-worn ski jackets— one pink and black and the other was blue—and the final was a small girl with big blonde curls and a light pink Care Bears parka with matching boots and knapsack. The girl was coming out of the washroom and had tears in her red-rimmed eyes.

"It's okay," the pale woman said, cooing while she held her arms wide.

"If we don't start a fire, we're dead," one of the big men said and the other big man said, "Yep, even if that radio ain't ruined, gonna be hours before anyone can get here."

The young man in the blue parka said, "What, we just sit here?"

"No. You climb your butts out that emergency door and start bringing in luggage. We'll need to hunker down," one of the big men said.

Jordan stood up then and nearly fell, his body

pitching and his knees going to noodles while his arms instinctively latched onto a seatback before him. He was woozy as hell. His hand followed another instinct back up to his head and he winced against the pain of touching that fresh wound. The pale woman across the aisle licked her lips, or at least Jordan thought she did, though when he looked again, she was cradling the child against her chest, singing gently, "*Take, these broken wings and learn to fly again, learn to live so free.*"

One of the big men put his meaty hand on Jordan's shoulder from behind. "There'll be a first-aid kit up there. You just stay put 'til I get back inside. We'll be just a bit. Was a medic in the Congo back in 'sixty-three, so I know how to deal with this," he pointed to Jordan's head, "and that," he pointed to the front of the bus and the destroyed bodies.

The mess was like a great metallic and rubber wound that wept a steady trickle of blood from between the shadowy cracks where it had enveloped all the passengers from the front half.

Jordan nodded and leaned back. A shiver ran up his spine, eyes were on him, and he looked at the woman again. "What happened, anyway?"

The woman ceased her rendition of Mr. Mister's *Broken Wings* and nodded out the window. Through the snow was a massive shadow in the moonlight, a halo of debris surrounding it. Jordan had to squint but then understood and drank in that they'd hit an ancient snowplow with an unreadable sign affixed to the giant blade.

"Driver lost control and spun the front end into that blade," the woman said. "He was moving too fast."

Jordan squinted tighter. "What happened to the driver?"

"He's dead."

"No. The driver of the plow."

The woman scrunched her mouth sideways. "Never ride this stretch?" she said and when Jordan gave his head a single, painful shake, she added, "Thing's from the 'forties. It's decorative. I'd bet that plow has been sitting on the side of this road for fifty years."

From the back of the bus came clanking sounds and whoomping sounds. Jordan turned, slowly. Every little movement sent painful bursts into his bones. The big man who'd been to the Congo had returned with a duffle bag of items in one hand and the first-aid kit in the other.

"We got lucky," he said and dropped the bag on the seat next to Jordan. "Someone was planning for the food prices in Fort 'Mac."

"Food prices?" Jordan said.

"Yeah, so they packed themselves a feast."

"Think we'll be here that long?" Jordan said, a whine creeping into his voice.

"Never know up here," the man said and as if to accent the point, an Arctic gust whistled through the destroyed bus. The man got busy with his work then.

The duffle bag on the seat next to Jordan had an open zipper and revealed several packets of Keebler cookies, dozens of individually wrapped Slim Jim meat sticks, two jars of Skippy peanut butter, a jar of Smucker's strawberry jam, and three boxes of Ritz crackers. Jordan saw it all and then saw none of it the moment the man touched his forehead, and an incredible flash of pain spotlighted his mind and drove him from consciousness.

—

"Where's the other guy?" Jordan said after he awoke, feeling much better. Daylight had risen, but the snowstorm left the skies a cold steely gray and the windows of the bus spackled with sticky fluff.

The big man remaining, the medic who'd been to the Congo, shook his head gently. "I suppose he went out to find help, but I can't figure it. Dale, he knows better. He knows where we are. Can't just walk a little ways and wave down a passing car; there's nobody and nothing out here."

"What?" Jordan said, frowning deeply enough that a skin cavern formed between his bushy eyebrows. "Then…why?"

The big man shook his head slowly, his eyes downturned, his motions melancholy. Beyond him and Jordan, the atmosphere on the bus was frosty enough that each exhalation hung on air and noses were steady taps. Everyone was miserable and pale. A small fire burned colorful flames between the seats and someone had hung articles of clothing from the ceiling, making a wall, hoping to trap more of what little heat they mustered with the fire. But the chill was so thorough it seemed to suck every invisible wave of comfort from the vicinity.

The woman remained with the little girl, cradling her in a way that suggested motherhood, though Jordan doubted that was the case. The two young men in ski jackets sat next to each other directly in front of the washroom, and the remaining big man sat behind

Jordan.

"He's gone. No trace," the big man said, still on the topic of his missing buddy.

The little girl stretched out her arm and held a pack of Keeblers toward Jordan and said, "You want a cookie?"

Jordan didn't pause for thought and reached into the bag, finding that he was indeed very, very hungry. As he munched the sweet, fudgy cookie, a realization set in, again also thinking of the big man's missing friend. "He'll die out there? How far are we from Fort McMurray?"

"Too far," the woman said. She held a jar of peanut butter but wasn't eating. "You'll need your strength." She passed the Skippy across the aisle.

Jordan accepted the food, again. Nobody else was eating then. All were somber, lost in thoughts and the worry wrote lines into every face, including the child's.

"Did the radio...?" Jordan began and looked behind him, between the seats, but trailed as the big man shook his head.

The child piped in, "Nobody can get us in the snow."

Jordan sighed. He dipped his index finger into the Skippy and brought out a glob of creamy peanut butter. It went into his mouth, saving him from having to say anything, saving him from the taste of this predicament.

———

"I need air," Jordan said. He rose and squinted against the acrid cloud hovering above them. The bus sometimes became smoky enough to make eyes water and throats burn—they'd gotten used to breathing in the tainted air as far as their lungs were concerned.

"I'm coming, too," the man in the blue ski jacket said, pointing out an icy window next to him. "The Northern Lights are going."

All turned or craned to see the flash of light muddied by the glass. Quickly then, as if this were a sign from God, perhaps a rescue timeline painted upon the sky, all within the bus paraded out the emergency exit at the back. Anything good was a welcome reprieve from the misery of not knowing if they'd ever get out of there. The step to the snowy road was far enough that after Jordan landed, he turned on his heels to help the child down. She was incredibly light, as if she were all coat and boots and backpack, no bones, fluid, or flesh. Once she had her footing, eyes pinned to the fantastic show above, Jordan offered help to the pale woman.

"Thank you," she said.

Her hands were very cold in his and the weight she leaned against him was confusingly opposite to the child, and he wasn't even lifting the woman. It was as if she'd dropped bags of cement against his arms. Enough so that she huffed as he stumbled away at the pressure when he lost balance and she had to quickly regain her footing or fall into the snow.

"Thanks," she said then; this time the sarcasm was heavy as their plight, heavy as her weight.

Jordan thought to say something, anything, but when the lights overhead danced a blast of green and blue, all other considerations departed. Like fireworks, the group craned their necks, though there were no oohs or ahhs. Right then, all that mattered were the lights—and in a bodily sense, the snot that had been flowing freely onto upper lips the entire time they'd been stranded. Which in turn demanded hands swipe at the tickling ooze.

Eventually the temperature conquered over entertainment. A thrumming shiver stole the moment's grace and buried it beneath frost. Jordan wrapped his arms around him, his hands numb—even within the thick brown mittens he'd pilfered from a dead person's pack. "Cold," he said and took off in a shuffle, back toward the emergency exit at the rear of the bus, passing the woman and the girl, as well as the two men in ski jackets. Jordan was surprised to find that the medic in the Carhartt was not already in the bus because he hadn't taken stock of him outside.

Within minutes, the child returned to the bus and offered Jordan the jar of jam, as if she was done with it and it needed put away, back in the pantry on a shelf she could not reach. The woman trailed the child inside; she had a chunk of deep red strawberry in the corner of her mouth. Jordan wiped his own mouth and she got the message and mimicked.

"So, what are you two doing once you get to Fort 'Mac?'" Jordan said as he set aside the jam and then knelt to stoke the fire—the men in ski jackets had unbolted two rows of seats sometime while Jordan slept and had started the fire directly on the steel floor of the bus. So far, they'd managed to keep from burning any integral part of the shelter.

"I just go where I'm told," the woman said.

Jordan was barely listening. With one hand he stoked the coals and fading flames and with the other he used the heat of his bare palm to melt ice from the interior of the window. "Told by who?" he said.

"The master," the woman said, and this had a little more of Jordan's attention.

"What?"

Before she had a chance to answer, the emergency door of the bus flew open and a great gust of cold air burst in, along with the men in ski jackets. One held two pieces of a snapped Titan hockey stick, making a cross. The other had a weighty claw hammer. The woman popped forward, hissing and slammed her shoulder into the one with the hammer, even as the hammer came down against her forehead.

The hideous thunk had Jordan recoiling and reaching for the child, pulling her tight to his chest. "What the hell's going on?" he shouted but was ignored.

The woman jerked her head back and then forward, viper-striking at the man's nose, before reefing away with her fangs clenched. The crunch of cartilage and the tearing of flesh were barely audible over the crackling fire and the whine of the man keeping distance, trying to use a makeshift cross as a shield. The woman swallowed her prize as her boney fingers dug into the exposed sinus of the man who'd struck. With each retreat to swallow, she swiped her tongue and her lips—so much blood, it almost looked like clown paint. The man's eyes rolled as she rooted toward the brain, cracking bone and ripping flesh as she went, grunting while slurping his life away.

"Lord, save us," whimpered the man with the broken hockey stick held before him—the word Titan split between the TIT and the AN. The man stiffened a moment, recognizing that the blade of the broken stick had been signed by Wayne Gretzky and was nothing short of a collector's item. A steady whine played up his throat, bemoaning the anguish of terror and then of waste.

The woman dropped the dead man and leaned over the corpse to press her lips to the hole she'd dug through his forehead. Her slurping seemed to silence the universe.

Jordan's lips moved in a *what the hell?* motion but no sound came of it. The little girl grasped at his arm tightly. The tips of her nails like fat needles trying to puncture his jacket. He squeezed her right back. He hadn't had sufficient time to consider that this monster and the little girl were a team of some sort.

The man with the hockey stick began mumbling a prayer but stopped abruptly. The *spirit* had taken him. He charged at the woman. The splintered ends of the stick's shaft became dual spears. He stabbed downward. One nailed heavily into the hood of her coat, doing no significant damage, while the other landed against her collar bone and slipped beneath the meat of her flesh. She bounced upright and the man fell backwards. He began crab-walking in reverse wearing an expression of total defeat—the *spirit* gone as quick as it had come.

The woman rose to her full height, black blood oozing from the puncture next to her neck. She took one step, two, three. The man matched her pace until he connected with the wall of the washroom. The woman lifted her arms as if aiming a chokehold, but then stopped. Her expression soured. The stick had gone through the chain of her necklace and the heavy ruby slipped down, down, down until it clunked on the floor. For three seconds, nobody breathed; even the fire seemed stilled.

The woman began to fall apart, her skin graying, becoming greasy fur as it tumbled in a wave of meaty rats with bright red eyes. The man screamed. Jordan gasped. The child held tighter, making his arm ache.

The rats broke loose from their womanly formation, blanketing the man in a writhing pelt. A pool of blood formed on the floor beneath him. The man swung and kicked to little avail. Soon enough, it didn't matter. The fur of the rats had started to gray and thin, sudden mange had clumps falling to the floor like fur balls dusted from a bookshelf, revealing endless wrinkles and sharp bone structures. Bite holes covered the man in a horrific canvass of dalmatian spots, but he was winning this horrendous battle. Hysterical laughter piped free of his mouth as he smashed the creatures into bony, furry Rorschach splotches.

"Got you! Got you!" he shouted as the blood splatters quickly solidified and became dust mounds, ready to be blown into oblivion. "Got you! Got you!"

The little girl let go of Jordan, and he tried to hold her as if she were the one in trouble here, but she pulled his arm aside with only a minor effort. She stepped into and then through the fire and to the ruby amulet. She picked it up and kissed the gem before pocketing it. Jordan watched in terror.

"Got you!" The man's voice had gone hoarse. "Got you." The thrill of victory falling away with the pure oddity of it all.

The little girl stepped through dust mounds and stood between the man's legs. He tried to push her away, as if to shield her from the blood, but she took his arm in her little hands and snapped it like a toothpick. The man screamed and lashed out. The girl dodged the punch and popped forward like a jack-in-the-box, slamming her mouth against the collar of the man's coat. Her little hands tore the flimsy material to shreds. The man rolled sideways, taking the girl from her feet, but never taking her from her focus. Once her teeth punctured skin, the man fell limp, puddling like so much snowmelt.

Jordan watched for as long as he dared while the child drank her fill, but it was after only seconds of slurping and spilled blood that he turned away and dropped into his seat. He scratched at the condensation ice on the window and looked to the sky. Beyond the dancing lights was a huge moon, maybe a night from being full, maybe two.

—

Jordan awoke to the child leaning over him. She had his wrist pulled to her mouth. He was numb, though not so numb that he didn't feel the depleting flow of his blood, not so numb that he couldn't move either. He jerked away the hand and the child tilted her head, giving him a *you think so?* expression. Blood trickled from the wound she'd bitten. He tried to fight for a moment when she reclaimed her meal, but he recalled the sound of that man's broken arm and just how simply she had made it happen.

Daylight, but overcast, he imagined the full moon would be upon them come nightfall. He needed that to be so, needed this time to pass.

—

"Eat," the child said, her voice gone husky, her

expression shifting ever so slightly. The childishness now remained only in physical appearance. "You need your strength. We start out tomorrow evening."

Jordan was lightheaded and tired. He scooped peanut butter onto Ritz crackers before popping them into his mouth and chewing through the dusty, dry wads. Out the window, the moon was full. He sincerely wished he were a werewolf.

Wasn't the werewolf a natural enemy, even predator to the vampire?

Every day he survived was a day closer to salvation. Had to be.

—

The child didn't feed on Jordan again, not yet. He had his energy up and needed it. The three extra layers he wore were heavy enough to make him sluggish, even at the beginning. The bag of food was not so heavy and even if it had been, he needed that. The sleeping bag was lighter yet, feeling like a feather on his shoulder. The moon overhead was plenty bright. Jordan imagined dog teeth tearing into the child as she tried to muscle through his supercharged wolf bones. Silliness. Werewolves didn't exist. He glanced up at the moon.

The child held a *Ghostbusters* flashlight in her bare hand, its yellowy beam cutting the shadows of the snowy road. She had a shovel in her other hand. She'd asked him many questions as time droned by and he didn't fight her; simply answered, and mostly honestly.

Now, growing near to sunrise, she said, "Stop. Dig us a cave in the snow." She pointed to the high bank at the eastern side of the road.

"If the sun hits you, you'll die, right?" he said as he unslung his pack.

"If the sun hits me, I get a sunburn and a very bad headache. The movies and books give too much hope for humanity. You're cattle and the sun is an irritation. Now, dig." She tossed the shovel to his feet.

"Take a chill pill," Jordan said, but got to work.

Before the overcast sun had a chance to aggravate the child, the pair were in the cave. Jordan lay in a stolen sleeping bag, atop a stolen foam rectangle. Only his left arm and his head remained in the frosty open air. The child had her mouth to his wrist. Drinking.

"Close to one thousand years and every now and then you taste something new. Your taste is something new," she said and licked her chops.

"Thank you?" he replied, eyes closed, welcoming whatever venom numbed him while she fed because he felt little of the chill in those moments. He watched out the cavemouth and wondered just how many days remained and if they were to be his last days.

"Very different," the child said after lifting her bloody mouth from the wound once again.

—

Slowly, with his head down to the wind, Jordan carried onward, glancing often to the sky as if the moon's clock could be pushed and the sun would rise sooner, letting him rest. It, of course, would not be rushed, especially in those northern climes, and Jordan gritted his teeth against the bite of the cold whipping wind. Sweat froze upon his brow and chilled deeply via an entry point at the collar of his coats. The loss of blood left him feeling exposed, as if he walked that stretch of desolate highway in only a t-shirt and linen pants.

"Are you going to kill me once we get where we're going?" he said, slowing.

"Keep pace," the child said. "I can do five days or more without food, surely I can make it without you if you continue to whine."

"Right," Jordan said, though he did not believe it, so he plodded, feigning weakness. To delay brought in possibilities, maybe. He was never really sure how all the rules of the universe worked, especially when it came to monsters in the real world, even when it came to the ones he was intimate with.

—

The wind had the snow swirling dervishes before them, but midway through the tenth night of walking, the lights of a distant town shined so impossibly close it seemed as if Jordan might reach out and touch them. But it was a trick, with the moon but a sliver of itself, those town lights grew long fingers. Jordan had to fight his legs to keep himself from pushing on too quickly.

"As soon as there's other food, you'll kill me," he said. Not a question.

"I could make you rats," the child said and after a pause added, "but your taste."

"Gag me with a snow shovel," Jordan said. His feet continued their swish, swish chorus and his face remained downturned, though his eyes glanced to the sky every few minutes. Hoping. Hoping.

As the sun played at the cusp of the eastern horizon, the child said, "One more night and you'll have a choice." She tossed the shovel down next to Jordan.

He stopped and turned to face the eventual sun. "What choice?" he said, dropping the food pack.

"You can become my servant, or I feast and share you with the wolves," the child said, candidly.

"Wolves?" he said, thinking about werewolves and how that felt like the only hope, at least while the moon was full.

"Those wolves," the child said, and the way her voice drifted on the wind, Jordan understood that she was looking behind them. He turned. Six very large wolves stood by, strangely cautious for predators on their natural hunting grounds. "I'll eat my fill and pass along your body."

"And I have until when to decide?" he said.

To Jordan, the wolves appeared to be licking their lips, their eyes lusty, their willingness to stay put ribbon thin. In this part of the world, beneath that steadily rising sun, man was at the bottom of the food chain.

—

Jordan ate all the food that remained. The child said nothing, focused fully on feeding herself instead. The plan was to get enough food into himself to soak whatever poison seeped through his body to numb him while she ate. Perhaps she'd miscalculate, perhaps he wouldn't sleep so soundly through the night.

"Sleep, food," the child said and curled up next to him, a blood moustache playing a smile onto her upper lip at the corners of her mouth.

Jordan rolled to his side and forced both hands,

bare flesh vulnerable to the elements, into the snowy wall next to him. He slept and slept and slept, but somewhere beyond the cavemouth, the sun was up. Before the sun was down, Jordan rose. The wolves had retreated, for now. Clumsily, with shovel in hand, he ambled along the highway as quickly as his legs would take him. The town was barely visible, even with the storm abating—twenty, twenty-five miles yet of flat, flat terrain.

Now he watched the skies, hoping to see nothing of the moon, knowing his salvation lay in its lack. It had always lay within its lack. Pure blackness held a promise of tomorrows. His breaths came out in ragged puffs as the hours passed. He'd put good distance between himself and the child. He was so close to town it would be entirely reasonable that someone might spot him; should the winds ease and the blustery drifts settle.

The sun had dipped all too quickly. Eleven minutes after it touched the western horizon—it couldn't be later than 3:00 PM—the light evaporated and left behind a rusty gray sky. The first wolf made itself known, growling one heartbeat before planting its great paws upon Jordan's back. He flopped forward, taking a mouthful of snow down into his lungs. The shovel had become useless.

Teeth latched onto two hoods of the coats he wore and began reefing Jordan's body like a ragdoll. Fighting was beyond him. He whined and took it, trying to watch the skies, trying to survive into a moonless night. Once the first wolf had him flipped, two others pinned him, one encircled his throat with its incredible jaws. Jordan swallowed a lump and awaited the inevitable.

But it didn't come, not yet.

He lay in the snow, six wolves right there, looking to feast, but not partaking, showing impossible restraint. Below the panting and whining of the dogs, footfalls approached. They then grew loud, the snow beneath the child's feet compressing beyond her physical weight, as if that snow understood her true mass.

"Did you really think I'd let you leave me?"

Jordan couldn't speak. His eyes remained on the sky, as if tied there.

"Tell me, what is it? That taste in your blood."

Jordan took a long blink. The black night was finally upon them. He'd set his leave to match the cycle of the moon so there wouldn't be any accidents, and had purchased a bus ticket accordingly.

"Tell me or I'll let them eat you while you breathe!" the child had replaced the wolf at his throat. "I've never tasted a man like you! Tell me and I shall—!"

"I'm not a man," Jordan said quietly. The black night was the cover his kind had used since the beginning of time. To stay immersed and invisible was to stay alive.

"Not a man?" The child straightened as she straddled Jordan's chest.

"Not…a…maaah!"

Electricity surged through Jordan's veins and he embraced the beauty that was transformation. There was no pain as the bones in his legs and arms elongated to more than twice their lengths. His chest tingled as it broadened and flipped the child away.

His muscles sang at their ballooning. His flesh danced as coarse white fur sprouted from his pores.

The child stood, watching, expression agog.

The wolves took to running.

Jordan's jawbones snapped and remolded, even as he stood and attempted to say *not a man*, but had the words come out in a grizzly triple tap roar. He pushed upright, the stolen clothing tearing and spilling from his form.

"You can't exist," the child said, disgusted.

Jordan reached his incredible yeti paws forth and slashed at the child. She leapt back, turning to sprint into the night, but the beast was already moving. Its great legs bent before springing, nailing the child from behind, sending her into the snow. She struggled, kicking and swinging, but she had no leverage. Jordan opened incredible, beastly jaws, steamy slobber raining over the child, and then he bit down. Cold, cold blood sprayed forth and the child wailed with a voice older than the construction of the Tower of Pisa as her dark life ended beneath an even darker night sky.

Jordan controlled himself and fell back; eating a vampire might be like eating ant poison. He looked to the empty sky and thanked the universe he hadn't had to wait another night for true black. A growling howl left the beast's mouth—human laughter passed through inhuman vocal chords—and Jordan decided, if he could catch them, that he'd dine on a wolf. Maybe two.

CHAPTER SIX
SISSY WHITE

A silence hovered over the crowd for about five seconds before Sissy gave a nervous laugh and a short bout of clapping. "You're crazy," she said. Since the incident, she'd been a nut for horror stories and didn't know why, not that she questioned it.

Maybe it was because of her mother. There were always Ramsey Campbell, and Thomas Tryon, and Charles Grant, and V.C. Andrews, and, of course, Stephen King novels lying around. She'd never picked up her mother's love for books, not the same way, but the horror seemed to have stuck. It had become especially important after the trauma.

"What's interesting to me," John said, "is that the sasquatch has gone, in the public eye at least, from a gentle mystery to a bloodthirsty monster. I've done a great deal of research on this topic."

"Here we go," Amy said.

"It seems the sasquatch, in general, has evolved into something new. Perhaps it's that we as humans have fanned out, into too much sasquatch territory, or it's a result of ecological changes making some foods harder to obtain. It's why I've done a little experiment—no, wait, I'm going last. Almost spilled my own beans," John said.

"Experiment?" Billy said.

"In due time," John said. "Now, who wants to go next?"

"I suppose I can go," Nancy said. "Mine's a little interactive this year. What none of you know is that the production company that financed the *Beastly Urges* series previewed the first movie and told me to cut the opening scene, which was a prologue that stands alone. I'd never mixed it or mastered it, until recently. So, make sure you're on the resort's Wi-Fi with your phones and send me an email at Nancy H Director at Nancy H Director .com. I'll shoot you all a link to this rough little gem."

Fingers got to work.

"Incredible!" Billy said as he typed. "I love all the *Beastly Urges* movies!"

"So glad to hear it," Nancy said, doing well to hide the eyeroll in her words, though not entirely succeeding.

Sissy got out her phone as the others had and shot off an email. It was less than two minutes before she was linked and onto the private site hosting the video.

"Now, this is a live stream, so tell me when you're all ready and I'll hit play—keeps us from having an annoying echo while we watch," Nancy said.

"This is something," Freddy said.

Sissy nodded, waiting, hoping the movie wasn't too randy. Watching that kind of subject matter in public wasn't really her thing.

CHAPTER SEVEN
NANCY HARGENSON

Billy Bob Jones looked at the handful of rubbers his mother had slipped into his backpack and frowned. She was always so nosey. Besides, he'd never been an overly horny guy. What his mother didn't know, and neither did his girlfriend, was that he planned to wait until marriage. He wasn't religious or prudish, simply wanted it to mean the whole damned world. He put the condoms in the glove box and looked out the window.

Gary Ray Thompson was just stepping out of the gas station, slipping his wallet into a back pocket of his tight, tight jeans. He'd told Billy Bob that he'd picked them out because they showed off his package so well. Billy Bob looked anywhere but at his buddy's package because it always made him laugh; he stuffed.

Unlike him, Gary Ray seemed totally horned up and raring to go at all times. His only problem was that in about half the situations where he actually got a girl naked, she'd involuntarily laughed at his meager manhood. Now he had to date girls from out of county or ones who'd been homeschooled because his rep preceded him. Of course, none of that mattered now, not really. He'd been going steady with Crystal-Lynn for a month and he'd told Billy Bob that she said she loved him and had never been with anyone else. The fact they'd felt each other up every way they could suggested that perhaps she didn't mind a little less than average.

"The van is gassed and ready to break loose the juice," Gary Ray said as he hopped in behind the wheel and began humping at nothing, rocking the entire van. "We need anything else before we pick up the honeys?"

"Don't think so."

"Man, I'm finally going to give Crystal-Lynn the python," Gary Ray said as he wheeled the van onto the street.

Traffic was slow and thick. Friday afternoon of a long weekend in July. On the van's stereo was a song titled *Hypervigilant* by Creedence Bluewater Revival, a cover band with a handful of original songs they liked to sneak in now and then during live shows. Billy Bob tapped on the vinyl of his door, a little off beat.

"I sure hope Tiffany Amber doesn't get too drunk again," Billy Bob said.

They were about to become part of a log jam at a corner when Gary Ray swung the wheel and they launched into a Taco Bell parking lot. He then cut through the now vacant drive-thru and bounced onto a street adjacent.

"Geez, man!" Billy Bob said, gaining air from his seat when the van hit the new street.

"Man, we're going to party. We'll all be drunk. Get drunk and get naked," Gary Ray said and then tapped the faded air-freshener dangling from his rearview mirror—a woman wearing only bikini bottoms and a lack of tan lines up top.

Billy Bob shook his head gently. "I don't mind getting drunk or getting naked, it's just…Tiffany Amber, she really wants to make it, and I've only known her a week."

Tiffany Amber was a friend of Crystal-Lynn's from out of town. They went to a Catholic school and only chanced upon Gary Ray at first when he'd gone to the drive-in to see *Cube*. She had laughed the moment after she bent to give him a blowjob. He was used to it enough that when she suddenly got terribly frightened that he was going to hit her, he simply asked that she kindly vacate his vehicle by the time he returned from the refreshment stand. Tiffany Amber had had a boyfriend then when he introduced himself behind her in line to get popcorn. He slipped her his number, which was written on a sheet of paper he'd had readied beforehand. Tiffany Amber lasted only another week with the other boy before sheepishly calling Billy Bob.

The van cut a right and was suddenly looking at mostly open road out of town. Gary Ray gunned it, the speedometer dancing up to seventy.

"Hey, man, better slow down. If the cops catch us with this pot, we're toast," Billy Bob said.

"Cool out," Gary Ray said, but didn't slow. "You need to relax. Probably getting laid would do you some good."

Billy Bob looked out the window, scowling.

—

"I'm so ready to party!" Tiffany Amber said. She sat on stacked beer cases next to Billy Bob, who'd moved to the back once they picked up the girls. "I'm going to get wild. I'm just warning you," she said and reached between Billy Bob's legs and stroked his penis against his thigh.

He laughed it off. "Tons of time for that, babe," he said as he squirmed his manhood out of her reach.

"There it is!" Crystal-Lynn said as they passed a crude, hand painted sign that read: BONER RIDGE.

Gary Ray wheeled the van into the busy parking lot and put the shifter to P. "We're here and it's time to get wild!"

Crystal-Lynn and Tiffany Amber woo-wooed simultaneously while Billy Bob forced a poor excuse for a smile to his lips.

—

"Come on, baby," Tiffany Amber said, unbuttoning her thin plaid shirt to reveal unnaturally firm and unnaturally high DD breasts. "Just a quickie."

"I'm not...I don't..." Billy Bob said, unable to fight her off. She had his penis out, tonguing the glans and down the shaft. "Please...I just..."

"I can't wait to feel this hot meat rocket in my juicy pussy," she said before engulfing him with her mouth.

"Oh, God!" he said and spasmed.

"Already?" Tiffany Amber said, not so much in character as a splash of white ran up her cheek.

Billy Bob had wide eyes. "I do not want that yet," he said, seriously nervous looking.

Tiffany Amber looked askance to her left and then down to Billy Bob's shrinking penis. "Oh baby, that tasted so good. I can't wait until later." She raked a fingernail along her cheek to drag cum into her mouth. She made a practiced ecstasy face, like the load was the world's tastiest drink.

—

They sat around a campfire drinking cans of beer. It wasn't yet dark. There was a boombox playing a song titled *River of Love* by Creedence Bluewater Revival.

"I'm totally tipsy, and totally horny," Crystal-Lynn said when she sat on a blanket next to Gary Ray and Tiffany Amber.

"Me too," Tiffany Amber said from another blanket where she sat next to Billy Bob.

"Me three," Gary Ray said.

Billy Bob pushed to his feet. "We'll need more firewood," he said and started away.

"Now I'll get cold, can I sit with you guys?" Tiffany Amber said.

"Oh yes, let us warm you up," Crystal-Lynn said, rubbing at Tiffany Amber's chest and arms.

Billy Bob didn't look back. Almost immediately, he was beyond earshot of the group and standing alone amidst the tall trees of the forest, a clearing just ahead of him. He leaned against a birch tree with his head on his right forearm.

"What am I going to do?" he said.

"You're gonna party, that's what."

Billy Bob looked around. "Who said that?"

"Me."

"Me who?" Billy Bob said and began following the voice. He made it to the clearing and stopped dead, looking up in wide-eyed amazement. "Elvis?"

"That's right. Now, you're a hunka, hunka loving machine and you need to go back there and give those girls what they need," the huge face of Elvis said, looming from amid the clouds overhead.

"But I want it to mean something," Billy Bob said. "Those girls, they'll only want me for my fat cock."

"Sometimes you've got to give what you have to find someone to love you tender. Don't ask me why. If you don't, that's where the heartaches begin."

Billy Bob looked at his hands and then beyond to the erection bulging out the thigh of his blue jeans.

"Now go on back there and ask them ladies if they're lonesome tonight. You know Gary Ray isn't man enough to do it alone. They need that hound dog you got hiding in your pants."

Billy Bob began nodding. "Hey, yeah. Thanks, Elvis, I—" When he looked to the sky, it was empty. He spun and ran back toward the campsite.

—

Gary Ray lay back with his pants open. Two inches of hard pink flesh jutted out from his fly, looking a bit plastic. He had his eyes closed, almost wincing preemptively.

The girls were naked and rubbing one another's arms and breasts. Crystal-Lynn crawled over to Gary Ray then. Tiffany Amber's eyebrows lifted to her hairline as her friend mounted the man. She rocked and stopped. Rocked and stopped.

"It keeps falling out?" she said. "Isn't it supposed

to hurt my first time?"

Tiffany Amber laughed then. "Not with a baby carrot!"

Gary Ray's eyes opened, and a single tear slipped from the corner.

"Maybe this is big enough?" Billy Bob said, stepping back into the campsite, naked and stiff.

An expression of great shock overtook her face. "Look at those cocks!"

Billy Bob stopped and frowned. He turned and two towering sasquatches stood behind him, each had a package that made his look like Gary Ray's and Gary Ray's look like it belonged on a mouse.

The first sasquatch—the one with the Black member—grabbed onto Billy Bob's head and spun it as it reefed upwards. The blood sprayed in a perfect fountain as his suddenly wooden looking body dropped to the forest floor.

Gary Ray screamed and pushed out from beneath Crystal-Lynn, just in time for the sasquatch with the white member to reach down and pluck the small penis from the man like it was picking a strawberry from a shrub. Another blood geyser sprouted, and Gary Ray screamed. The sasquatch stretched the detached organ like rubber before dropping it.

"Please," Gary Ray moaned, his face red and smeary with tears.

The sasquatch bent and picked him up, his body floppy and disjointed as it flew through the forest.

"Look at those cocks," Tiffany Amber said again.

CHAPTER EIGHT
SISSY WHITE

"Weird as this is, it really sets up the entire franchise," Billy said, thoughtfully.

"Wait, so after that, they just have sex with the sasquatches?" Sissy said.

"To find out, you'll have to buy the new, anniversary boxset, featuring all the before lost footage," Nancy said and then laughed. "Yeah, that's the sum of it."

"People like it…I mean for…" Sissy said, trying not to cringe.

"Some must," Nancy said.

"It's really not bad. The story and the acting are better than average for that kind of movie," Amy said. "Most times there's not much effort put into it. If Nancy here were more into making movies for a majority, she'd probably be for real famous instead of sasquatch porn famous."

Sissy turned to look at Nancy again. She sitting up a bit straighter, taking this as a compliment rather than a critique on the kinds of movies she liked to make. The moonlight hit her in a way that made her look much younger than she was.

"I don't mean to be rude, but it's getting late and I have a little something planned before we go off to bed," John said.

"Your experiment?" This came from Freddy, the man with huge sideburns and big John Travolta in the 'seventies hair.

"In due time. How about you go next, Freddy?" John said.

"Yeah, okay. This story actually came from a guy who contacted me. I looked him up online and it turns out the deaths are completely traceable."

Billy whistled.

Sissy stiffened. This was one occasion where being the only member of a crowd was good. Nobody else needed to know someone who'd died for the grisly appetites of beasts.

CHAPTER NINE
FREDDY TALBOTT

Elizabeth Horner crouched with her elbows on her bare knees, watching the fluffy white rabbit at the edge of the woods. Behind her, distantly, she could hear her father talking to his strange friend, Henry. Henry was a hunter and went on and on about how dangerous the woods were, but Elizabeth, and her parents didn't think so. Every time Henry left, her mother swirled an index finger next to her temple while pulling a face and crossing her eyes.

Still, Elizabeth, being only nine, was not to go into the woods alone, and most times she obeyed unquestioningly. But this rabbit. It had a piece of plastic wrapped around its leg and was hopping awkwardly. It wouldn't do to leave it there.

She took three slow steps closer, still crouched. Her bright yellow sundress swished against the grass behind her. The rabbit hobbled in a frenetic burst of energy, the plastic causing it to veer to its right. Elizabeth stopped and stilled. The rabbit did the same but for its steadily twitching nose.

Seconds passed. Elizabeth took a half-step, creeping. And another, creeping. Another, creeping, creeping, creeping. The rabbit bolted and this time Elizabeth did the same. Her mind was consumed by the chase, not a thought was spared to the fact that she was not to go into the woods alone.

Quickly, she was out of breath, leaning with her hands on her knees. She'd run for how long? There was no way of knowing exactly, no way of knowing the direction she'd taken, for before the rabbit disappeared, it had bounded sporadically. She turned around then and recognized the folly. She started walking straight back, blind to the fact that straight was the last thing she'd walked to get out there.

—

Florence Horner stood over the stove, stirring the taco meat and seasonings. Behind her, Gil Horner had just said goodbye to his guest—Henry, the man with the strange ideas about the forest—and stepped up behind his wife.

"Smells good."

"Smells like meat and mix. Go grab Elizabeth," Florence said.

Gil kissed her cheek and turned away. The first stop was the den where Elizabeth spent too much time playing Nintendo or on her iPad. "Honey, supper's almost—" Gil stopped midway down the stairs. His daughter was not there. He went back up and down the long hall to the only pink door in the home. He pushed it open and the scent of candy-scented perfume hit him. The room was a mess, but Elizabeth wasn't there.

"Where'd you last leave her?"

Florence looked up from the glasses she was pouring water into. "In the backyard, but that was an hour ago. I figured she'd have come in by now."

Gil shrugged and stepped out onto the back deck that stood above a stone patio below and overlooked the yard, all the way to the forest. They had two acres of land total and it appeared Elizabeth wasn't outside, not on the rear two-thirds of them anyway. The first threads of worry began to stitch his mind. He hurried back through the door.

"She not there?" Florence said.

Gil didn't answer, he went to the garage door and then outside to the front yard. Not a soul stirred but for a couple ravens perched on the stone birdbath. He scrunched his face, thinking. She wouldn't have gone into the forest, surely.

He pulled his phone from his pocket and opened the motion-sensor app that went with the cameras he'd let Henry install—so long as he had access to see all the critter activity too. Three different cameras caught motion close to an hour earlier. A rabbit. Elizabeth.

"Dammit," he said, still thinking he could easily pinpoint the girl. Eventually she'd trip another camera and he could hurry to it.

"She went into the forest?" Florence said, turning off the heat and covering the meat with a glass lid.

"Yeah, she chased a rabbit. Better come with me. She triggered three cameras. We'd better be close out there for whichever she triggers next."

"That girl," Florence said and untied her apron.

"Grab your phone. I'll head west and you can—"

Gil frowned. "I'll go left and you go right. She won't be far."

Florence playfully stuck out her tongue, though signs of worry creased her brow.

—

A camera more than a mile from the property line was triggered and recorded Florence and Elizabeth walking hand-in-hand. Gil watched it and then sent a text. He geo-located the camera with the GPS app on his phone. He followed, watching the screen as much as watching his feet. No response came from Florence, and that was not really a surprise.

Minutes passed. Distantly, a crack echoed out loudly through the forest. It was almost like a gunshot, but it carried the undeniable notes of broken wood. A single scream followed directly behind it.

Gil ran, cutting through the forest to an estimation of where his wife and daughter ought to be. He reached the camera they'd triggered and veered back toward home. He called out constantly, both their names. He heard nothing in return.

He got close enough to see the grass of his backyard and turned around, rushing, frantic, totally panicked. More than an hour had passed since he'd heard the crack. Sweat dripped and ran. His hands were slick around his quickly dying cellphone.

"Florence! Where are you?"

When he finally found them, he nearly tripped over their thrashed bodies, nearly slipped into the pool of blood that filled the indent of the forest floor beneath them. Both of their skulls had been cracked open.

CHAPTER TEN
SISSY WHITE

Sissy couldn't bring herself to ask why he thought it was a sasquatch attack, but John did. He was on the edge of his seat, seemingly starved for this kind of tale.

"There's no doubt in my mind or this Henry's mind. He's the one who contacted me," Freddy said. He paused dramatically to take a drink from a can of Diet Pepsi.

"Why though?" Amy said.

"Ahhh," Freddy said after swallowing. "Because, like I said, both their craniums were cracked…and their brains had been removed."

Sissy let out a long wheeze of pent breath. She could hear that horrid slurping sound now. The gristly chewing. Her heart pounding as she hid while sasquatches feasted.

"They don't?" Nancy said.

"Oh, yes, they do," Freddy said.

"In some areas, they've always done it. More and

more, the taste for brains has been spreading. That said, it appears that the males of any sasquatch family seem to have a stronger affinity for brains. At least according to what I've been able to gather from noted incidents throughout time. The best information is the most recent, and recently, sasquatches have been abandoning the solitude of mystery and encroaching on the peripheries of the modern world." John spoke with such conviction it was impossible to disbelieve him.

"You'd think someone would've captured one then, if they're being more…whatever," Nancy said.

"Who though?" Sydney said.

"It would have to be someone knowledgeable and equipped. Someone with patience," John said, a smile playing around his words.

"Why do you say it like that?" Sydney said.

John didn't answer, instead said, "Amy, I believe it's your turn."

"You all know me. I have no personal experiences."

Sissy frowned. This night was weird all around and not anything like what she'd expected, not that she really knew what she'd expected.

"You have something, though?" Billy said. "Something as extravagant and unbelievable as Sydney's story?"

"It was a story, one to tell at a campfire. I'd say out of all of us, I'm the only one who really nailed the theme here," Sydney said.

"Gentlemen," John said. "Please, Amy, go on."

"This can't leave this circle, but, premiering September twenty-eighth, exclusively on Shudder, season two of Underworld Gallery features yours truly in a segment titled *Hunger of the Beast!* My character's named Robyn."

Sissy sighed inwardly. Phony stories were so much more pleasant than real deal trouble. Outside of sharing her own story—for which she was contractually obligated to do—she didn't think she could stomach any more factual sasquatch terror.

Amy pulled out her phone. "It opens in a deserted five-star hotel in the middle of a Japanese forest. All little tables and blue wallpaper and dust on everything. Four urban explorers who specialize in abandoned places set down their packs and ready for a night a million miles from anywhere…"

CHAPTER ELEVEN
AMY SNELL

A gentle breeze played through the lobby of the Mountain Royal Hotel, making the moldy and drooping ceiling fans sway gently. Dust and forest debris littered the marble flooring in a way that made every footstep crunch while also leaving behind proof of their presence. If that was the sum of their impact, this trip would be a win.

"Pretty amazing no taggers have gotten in here," Bruce said. He was a fit thirty-something with a hiking backpack and a video camera.

"Hopefully the perfection of this place keeps it that way," Robyn said. She was the eldest of the group and was by far the most experienced of the hikers. She'd been hired to guide the trio to and through the ruins. Getting there had been simple, though arduous: picking them up at an airport, a day on trains, a half-day on buses, and finally nine miles down a foregone road that cut through a forest busy with life and myths. "I've been here six times, and I never tire of seeing it. Even with the little bits nature reclaims from season to season."

"Yeah…well, the light's getting low and I don't want to be wandering around in the dark, so how about you show us where's a good place to sleep and then tomorrow we moon over all the rotten shit?" Duncan said. He was Bruce's boyfriend. Trim, fit, but did not take to hiking that far. Up until this trip, the longest he'd ever walked was through an afternoon.

"Why'd you come if you don't want to see the hotel?" Bridget said.

She was Bruce's sister. She was short and stout, had to jog sometimes to keep up with the group, which made her sweaty and more disheveled than the others. Not a word of complaint had left her lips. She was closer to Robyn's age than the boys. This, and their shared sex, automatically paired them. Whenever they'd taken breaks, Bridget and Robyn chatted, split snacks, and looked at photographs together.

This pairing had been pleasant for everyone. Duncan hated Bridget. Bridget hated Duncan.

"There's a set of stairs to the second-floor. The interior rooms are holding up the best, though nothing is perfect. You may hear animals. You may even smell them or see them, but there's nothing that can hurt you here…outside tetanus or a hard fall," Robyn said as she started toward the far end of the lobby where the shadowy telephone booths stood in a long dormant row.

The evening sky shined redly through high windows. The marble stairs were fine enough that a touch of polish continued to shine through the dust.

The second floor had royal blue carpets and blue striped wallpaper. A couple of the rooms they passed, on the outer side of the building, had windows and walls broken in, where the elements had taken over: trees, bird's nests, and endless rot that creeped a little further with every passing second. In some places, the floor was soggy and soft underfoot, the heavy carpet being the only thing keeping the explorers from falling through those spots. They were easy enough to detect thanks to a change in coloration.

"There's a story that Eli Wallach was the last guest to sleep in two-one-nine," Robyn said, pointing into a room. The table had collapsed, and grass was growing from a chair cushion.

"Who?" Bridget said.

"Some rich Jew, obviously," Duncan said.

"Don't be so catty," Bruce said.

Robyn answered Bridget. "I suppose, dependent upon how you saw it, Eli Wallach was either the bad or the ugly—certainly wasn't the good—from that old Clint Eastwood movie. He did a lot of westerns and then TV later in his life."

"Oh," Bridget said.

"I don't know how anybody would be sure he was here, but since the story's him and not someone more significant or flashy, it lends some credence to it. I mean, if the story was that David Bowie was the last guest, it's instantly a little more suspect." Robyn rounded a corner and they moved deeper into the hotel, to places rot had yet to touch. "Okay. Most sleep in one of the first five rooms along the south wall here." She reached out her right hand and patted a doorframe.

"We're not all sleeping in the same room," Duncan said, his tone oozing attitude.

Robyn sighed. "Do what you like. I'll take this one. There's room for more, as I recommend sleeping on the floor. Beds are the first place critters seem to nest. So, there's space in here." She grabbed her flashlight from a belt loop, unhooking the clip with practiced skill, and pulled at the top. A plastic cover slid down and the flashlight became a mini lantern.

The room looked like most others, aside from the sparseness and cleanliness. The furniture had all been shoved to a wall, along with a boxy tube TV and musty linens. Robyn dropped her pack and turned, jumping with surprise.

"Hey, cool if I crash in here? Getting a bit spooky." Bridget held her pack in front of her.

"Yep, no problem. I had meant to tell you, it's customary to go outside for bodily functions."

"Customary?"

Robyn shrugged. "We are trespassing, so people can do what they want, it's simply a courtesy to the next explorers."

"Oh, yeah, makes sense. I've never done an overnight like this," Bridget said, bent over her pack to unlatch her sleeping bag.

"It's best to keep things simple…though I can't go without coffee in the morning, and since I have a pocket-sized camp stove, I also bring hot chocolate mix. Care for one, after we've settled in?" Robyn said.

"I'd like that."

———

"I don't know why you always have to be so

bitchy to people," Bruce said. "Especially my sister."

"Ugh," Duncan said, rolling his eyes.

They were on the floor in a room two down from the women. Bruce had lit a canned portable campfire and was taking selfies and self-facing videos with the light flickering against his skin.

"It's not even just my sister. It's like you hate all women," Bruce said.

"So? Women are stupid."

Bruce frowned, still shooting video. "You hang out with Lisa and Jenny, like, constantly."

"And they're dumb. They think we're girlfriends; I give them their little bit of cred' and they buy me cute stuff. I've never once shown either of them any respect, they deserve to be treated like garbage for not standing up for themselves."

"Why are you like this?" Bruce said, sighing out the final two syllables.

"Like what? It's all true."

The moments stacked until they became a minute, two minutes. Bruce finally asked, "Why did you even come with us?"

Duncan held up his phone. "Content, duh? I have to make brownies, is there like a toilet or something?"

"You have to go outside."

"Ugh, how about no." Duncan clicked on his flashlight and rooted through his bag for a roll of biodegradable toilet paper.

"It's common courtesy to future explorers to go outside. That's like rule number one."

"I'll go outside adjacent, okay?" Duncan was out the door before Bruce had a chance to say anything else. He hurried down the hallway, back the way they'd come. The stir-fry he'd taken away from the airport—against Bridget's suggestion…she told him to eat nuts and granola and berries and vegetables—was circling his guts like someone had pulled his drain plug. He went straight into the rotten room at the corner and crept along the wall, avoiding obvious weak spots. He set the flashlight down on its base, the beam shining a blue sphere onto the ceiling. He then got to unbuckling his pants, rushing it, the impending evacuation seeming to sense a countdown. He bent at the knees, bare butt hanging over a precipice created by a tree falling through a window and part of a wall.

"Oh, child," Duncan moaned as a hot rush spilled from his backside. "Lord, child."

Six machine gun sprays fired free from his ass, and his knees began to wobble, his body experiencing that unique euphoria a moment after that particular kind of terror has passed. He stretched for the toilet paper roll. Grabbed it and made a white mitt. He reached back to wipe and bumped something unexpected.

The surface was like thick hair and he immediately assumed a spider web. He gagged, had a miniature convulsion. The trick would be to keep balance and composure without getting any shit on himself. He began straightening. That spider web grew clawed fingers that grabbed either side of his waist. Duncan tipped back, dropping through the opening and to the trees below, his chin striking a stacked piece of furniture leaned against the outer wall. His vision went woozy and he blinked in and out of consciousness.

He came to fully on the overgrown lawn, looking up at the massive, egg-shaped head of a sasquatch, one wearing his diarrhea like Olay, anti-aging serum. He opened his mouth to scream.

A furry fist slammed between his jaws and tore free the back of his throat with a splash even hotter than the stir-fry had been departing his ass. His dying moments were spent watching this massive beast lift his uvula with two fingers and slurp it away like a shucked oyster.

———

Bruce was alone only a few minutes when he decided he needed to talk to Duncan, before his mind fully calmed and made excuses for his partner's attitude and behavior. He'd tell him it was over, and once they got back to civilization that Duncan had to get his stuff out of Bruce's home. It was stupid to think this trip would show Duncan another side of life, help cure him of his flimsy, one-dimensional view of people, and the world in general. The relationship was a wash and there was no time like right this second, here in this dark and moldy hotel, to tell him.

"Duncan?" Bruce said, whisper-yelling it. "Where are you?"

He reached the room Duncan had gone into and stopped. The light remained on the floor, as did Duncan's pack. The man himself was not there. The hole through the wall and floor looked alarmingly fresh. Bruce stepped gingerly across the room, sniffing at the faint shit smells—Duncan had definitely been here.

"Duncan?"

Bruce went as far as he dared and looked down into the hole. Moonlight shined through the structural damage of the hotel, glinting wetly off small black puddles that trickled away.

"If he fell, he'd…" Bruce trailed, thinking aloud.

If Duncan had fallen, where was he? He'd be in a pained heap down there, likely sobbing and cursing Japan, the Japanese, and Bruce for bringing him on this trip.

Bruce had to go down to see, but the last thing he wanted was to Andy Dufresne his way through the potentially shit-smeared hole.

He leaned in closer to say, "Duncan, if you're hurt, I'm coming around to find—"

A huge, humanoid hand reached from a shadow, its fur glistening like a dog's coat after a rainstorm. The wet stuff was dark, dark, dark. And the smell. It was like an abattoir dumpster on a warm day. And those eyes, spaced widely enough to suggest a massive head.

These attribute notes processed in a tenth of a second. The next thought was nothing as panic overcame him and the broken and rotting world below started rushing toward his face. That hand had grabbed him by the jacket.

He landed hard enough to whoosh the air from his lungs. He gasped, braying like a goat. He kicked and thrashed, working his limbs through the dusty rubble of the hotel wall and pieces of broken and moldering furniture.

Over him stood a sasquatch. His mind accepted this as quickly as it had acknowledged the new sensory inputs in the moment before being pulled through the hole. The sasquatch dropped straight, planting its knees on Bruce's shoulders. He remembered a video he'd seen about silverback gorillas, and he went still, non-threatening, which wasn't easy without having sufficient air in his lungs—would've been tough with enough air to whistle Dixie. The sasquatch touched his face, trailing a single claw up to his forehead.

Bruce inhaled deeply, finally. He managed to say, "Please, get off," before the sasquatch stabbed the claw into the bone of his forehead, sending out a spider web rattle as the bone fractured down several dozen lines. Bruce began to convulse, his mind now a pink and gray place of soft but painful hues. The last thing he felt was a wonderful warm liquid pool around his head like a halo, a baptism.

—

"What was that?" Bridget said. She had the hot chocolate mug in her hands about three inches beneath her chin, close enough that the scent was steady.

Robyn set down the collapsible mug from her pack, the dregs of the hot chocolate splashing thickly, almost like molasses. "I'll go see. Probably they went outside to…you know, and knocked something over."

"Hope so," Bridget said.

Robyn pushed to her feet. She unclipped a secondary flashlight from her belt and left the room with measured steps. Bridget thought about how wise that was, being so careful even when everything seemed okay about the hotel. If they'd met in a different situation, and also not way the hell in Japan, she thought they might've made good friends. Probably they'd have to settle with being Instagram contacts. Once she got back on some Wi-Fi, she'd toss over a follow and hope one was volleyed back.

Thinking of it, she got out her phone and snapped a handful of quick selfies. As she was pocketing the device, she heard her brother's voice far down the hall. Another crash followed. She trailed into the hallway and took a moment, decided to head away from the room Bruce and Duncan had chosen. The sounds really seemed to have come from the other direction.

Light shined through a doorway and Bridget peeked inside. "Bruce?" she said. There in the room was a mystery. A pack, a light, but no boys. She followed Robyn's example and stepped gingerly toward the hole in the wall where a window had once been. She looked down and deep black eyes looked up at her from a sopping mass of fur.

"Hell no," she said and stumbled over her feet as she attempted a panicked retreat.

The beast leapt up and grabbed the floor. It began pulling itself through—wood cracking, nails creaking, Bridget's heart reaching spin-cycle. She shuffled, the heels of her hiking shoes slipping over the dusty carpet. The sasquatch was up high enough to use the ledge of the hole like a seat. Bridget flopped over, took two crawling steps toward the door before claws dug into her calf. She screamed and reached from the yawning door, hooking her right hand, all the way to the punching knuckles, beneath the door.

"Robyn! Help!"

The sasquatch flipped her, snapping her leg at the knee. Bridget wailed, the bones of her hand had broken as well and remained lodged beneath the door. The sasquatch began reefing on the broken leg.

"Robyn! Ah! Ah!"

The thick cotton tore as the flesh beneath tore. Below the knee of her left leg was gone. The sasquatch held it like a corn cob and began chewing the meat from the bones, spinning it as it cleaned away the delicious flesh.

Woozy, Bridget reeled her arm like a tape measure, the broken bone in her hand screaming with signals, though drowned out by shock. Nothing hurt. She kicked with her legs, the patella of her left leg fell to the floor and the sasquatch snatched it like a special treat and sucked on it.

"Bridget!" Robyn said from the hallway.

"Help," Bridget said, crawling, almost oozing through the door.

———

A wet, chewing, smacking of gums sound played through the hallways, and it was horrible, disgusting, it drove dread needles beneath her skin. Robyn cringed. She knelt to help Bridget and finally saw the sasquatch. It saw her too. The sasquatch tossed the bones of its appetizer and pushed closer to Bridget on its hands and knees. A heavy palm clamped down on the center of Bridget's back and a lung burst from her mouth like toothpaste from a tube.

Robyn stumbled as she turned to break from the scene. The sasquatch leapt after her with tremendous force, crashing into the wall opposite of the hallway. Robyn began running. Spreading cracks in the plaster kept pace with her as the old hotel crumbled.

Ahead, the end of the hallway seemed to shake, though she couldn't be sure. The risk wasn't worth it. She hooked a right into the room she'd selected for the night. She spun immediately and pushed at the door, the carpet rolling beneath, refusing her effort.

"Fuck!" Robyn shouted.

She spun again. Her pack. The little campfire can. Bridget's pack. Behind her, the sasquatch growled, slamming a furry palm against the door, sending it open in a lightning wash of dust and slivers. Robyn fell to her knees. She felt the beast's breath on her neck as she grabbed for the little fire. She spun a third and final time, launching the can into the sasquatch's chest. The greasy fur lit like gasoline on water. It wailed and fell to its fours, thrashing and bouncing as the flames engulfed its pelt. It charged across the room, lighting the dried old wallpaper up like it had been awaiting a match all along. The flames devoured the crunchy paper and dusty glue beneath, spreading hungry fire in every direction.

Before Robyn had a chance to adjust to the idea of a blazing sasquatch chasing around a hotel room, she was at the eye of a firestorm. Sweat bubbled and ran. She covered her ears; those beastly wails were incredible, awful. The beast, though dying, finally refocused on Robyn. It bent its spine, chest barreled forward, head back, and mouth open to reveal a set of fantastic teeth; it screamed. It then lowered, knees bent, and leapt at Robyn. She dove sideways and the beast slammed through the wall, spreading the flames before doubling back.

This time, Robyn wasn't waiting to see what the sasquatch would do before taking action. The door out was burning, and if the flame had caught beyond…that floor didn't stand a chance. She ran to the far wall, cowering behind a burning love seat sofa sitting on its end. The sasquatch raged, burning by her. She scurried in behind it and through the hole. A massive sliver caught her calf. She hopped. She staggered. She limped. She was in a new room. It was on fire as well, but barely. She broke for the open door.

The beast barreled back into the new room just as she had exited. Robyn glanced over a shoulder as she ran along the unfamiliar hallway—big parts of the hotel had been blocked off: reasons unbeknownst to any urban explorers. As the wallpaper burned, the black hallway lit. Robyn gasped, swallowing down a scream as she discovered why this part of the abandoned hotel had been locked so tightly.

Bodies in dusty Mountain Royal Hotel uniforms. Skin like rotten leather, eye holes empty, fingers chewed off by the plump, uncaring rats living like kings and queens, creatures befitting the name of the resort.

The sasquatch roared. The flames continued to burn upon the beast's back, the heat and damage finally taking a toll on its speed. Robyn carried on. Into the darkness. The rats raced by her, finally shaken by the activity around. Moonlight poured in through a window at the end of the hallway.

Robyn slowed, looking for other options. She saw none. The sasquatch continued behind her. She closed her eyes, lifted her hood over her head, put arms out before her, and sprinted. The window came at her faster than she expected and barely jumped in time to clear the ledge and catch air. The ground was suddenly right there.

Splash!

She inhaled gamey green water before bursting upright like a swimsuit model. Thick slime clung to her flesh and clothing. She was terrified and shocked, but she was physically fine. She'd landed in the great fountain centering the front entrance's turnaround and drop-off.

Above, the flaming sasquatch roared before dropping from the window, nailing its head against the stone lip of the fountain. Its neck bent at an un-survivable angle. Robyn stumbled, dragging her pained leg over the lip of the fountain and to the dry asphalt below. The flames had begun lighting in the third and fourth floors. Unbroken glass shattered. The wood of the walls creaked. Air pockets popped.

Robyn lay flat, catching her breath, thinking it would be a long trek back and that she'd never be able to tell a soul. If she didn't die of hypothermia.

"Have to dry out before leaving," she mumbled.

Robyn pushed to her feet and shuffled to the dead sasquatch. It had big, deep eyes. If an animal had ever harbored a soul, it was this animal.

"Perhaps someone will find you someday and—"

Above the snap, crackle, pop of the fire, tree branches swished. She glanced to her right to see a massive beast step free of the forest. She jerked to her left: two more sasquatches. More and more, dozens of the incredible cryptids converged on Robyn and the dead beast. She turned. Directly behind her, a swarm of monsters.

She stilled in terror and waited, and waited, and waited.

CHAPTER TWELVE
SISSY WHITE

"Then what?" Billy said.

"Then whatever. It's up to the viewer. If they want her to live, the sasquatches let her go. If they want her to die, they ate her, maybe barbequed her body over the flames of the burning hotel," Amy said.

"That's no ending," Billy said, sneering.

"Sure it is," Sydney said. "Ends like a short story. TV's at its best when it mimics literary styles. If you ask me."

"Well nobody did, did they?" Billy said.

"Billy," John said.

Sissy studied Billy's face, trying to understand. Then it hit her. His true story was nothing on these fictions. Even if he'd love them later, he hated them now because they bettered his efforts. Sissy felt sorry for him. This was his life, his passion, and all but John and Freddy were asked to be here though never took the obsessive needle that pushed a hobby into an addiction. He'd probably sacrificed so much of his life hoping to experience a true face to face encounter and had never actually seen anything close to what she had.

He could have her story. If she could give it away and leave no trace, he could have it. Simple swap. She'd get Lyla and Derrick back in the process, of course.

"I had a friend visit a hotel in real life like the one you described," Nancy said, as if none of the irritation floating around the campfire had any impact on conversation. "She said it was equal parts incredible and sad."

"Sad because there were no yetis?" Sydney said, smiling.

Billy clicked his tongue against the roof of his mouth.

"Such a waste, I guess. Everybody's left it alone and it's all just out there moldering. Not only stuff and materials, but the hard work that went into building it. Somebody probably slaved over creating the designs and it came to life briefly and now it's simply dead," Nancy said.

"Sounds like you're describing trying to have a writing career," Sydney said.

"Or an acting career," Amy said.

Sissy ping-ponged her head listening. With each word that passed, she knew she was getting closer to having to tell her story. Her guts were on a ship at rough sea.

"Creatives are such whiners," Freddy said.

"Sure are," Billy said.

"Okay. I think we'd better reel it in. I guess it's time we get to Siss—" John said, and was cut off by

Sissy.

"Can I have another beer?"

"Certainly," John said, rising and stepping to the much-ignored cooler. He let the lid drop closed after grabbing another can. "Here." He handed it off and returned to his seat.

Sissy nodded, cracked the tab, and chugged half the beer. Immediately, an ice cream headache stabbed into her sinus. She squinted, waiting for the pain to abate, knowing all eyes were on her. Once it had numbed, she slugged the remainder of the can back. She burped. Twice.

The group sat in silence. Distantly, an animal howled to the moon. John finally cleared his throat and said, "Well, Sissy, that leaves you and me, and I'm going last. So it's you. Time to hear your—"

"Can I have another beer?" Sissy said.

Freddy reached into the inner pocket of his heavy Carhartt jacket and withdrew a beat-up silver flask. He reached over to Sissy. "Take it. More punch than beer."

Sissy took it and spun the cap. The taste was a surprise. She'd expected whisky or rum. It was lemon-flavored—more like hinted at—gin. She opened her mouth wider and let the cool burn trail inside until she had enough that her face felt on fire. She lowered the flask and barked a hiss. "Still need the beer."

John acted quickly. Sissy felt his eyes the most as she drank the beer.

"You ready?" he said, once she was about halfway through with the can.

Sissy took a deep breath, then another mouthful of

beer.

CHAPTER THIRTEEN
SISSY WHITE

Though she wasn't exactly sad, Sissy wiped the last remnants of tears from her eyes. The trip would have to be like the old days, just the three of them. It seemed since forever now that she, Lyla, and Derrick had been a singular unit. They hung out less now into adulthood but remained that kind of tight that was hard to come by. The kind most people never knew outside a marriage.

The camping trip was to give Lyla and Derrick a chance to get to know her boyfriend. Now, here and last minute as she awaited her friends, Pete had called her and said he couldn't make it, or rather, didn't want to make it. She and him had been forcing it since the beginning. Sissy called him an asshole, though he'd been right.

Given enough years stacked atop one another, relationships could begin to feel like life or death: how old could she get and still attract a half-decent mate? Probably as old as it took, but in the lonely nights by herself in her apartment, she took routes down the boulevards of paranoia and self-loathing.

It didn't help that her family growing up featured two perfectly suited people, ones who met in their early twenties and didn't have a child until they were getting close to forty. They'd died two years earlier in totally unrelated fashions: stroke, brought on by neonatal diabetes, and septic shock, from an untreated blood infection. If it weren't for Lyla and Derrick, she'd have nobody at all.

The intercom buzzer buzzed, and Sissy ran to the washroom to splash water on her face. She grabbed her two packs—one filled with clothes and camping gear, while the other had enough food to feed her for three extended weekends rather than one.

"Where's Pete?" Lyla said.

Sissy looked up from the packs she was stowing in the hatchback and didn't have to say anything.

"Oh…look, maybe it doesn't feel like it now, but that's a relief," Lyla said from shotgun.

"I know," Sissy said.

"Getting dumped sucks the big one," Derrick said, though he'd only been dumped once before and that happened in the ninth grade.

Out of the three of them, Sissy was the only one with any real dating experience. The kind that was mostly uncomfortable and consistently nerve-wracking. She'd done blind, speed, internet, and the bar scene; none of it was nice.

Sissy closed the hatch and climbed in behind Lyla because Derrick was tall enough at the wheel to eat up most of the foot room on that side. They rolled in quiet, Adele's *River Lea* single had just dropped and seemed to play on a loop. She leaned her head against the glass, mouthing along to the words.

"I know we weren't going to, but now that's it's only the three of us, should we stop at a liquor store?" Derrick said.

"Absolutely," Sissy said.

Lyla looked back through the crack between her seat and the door. "Pssst, you okay?"

"Yeah, I'm just being an emo baby. It'll pass by the time we get the fire lit," Sissy said.

Derrick pulled into Doug's Liquor Barn and killed the engine. "What do we need?"

"Nothing hard. I can see drinking myself into oblivion and getting even worse...going *mega* emo baby," Sissy said.

Lyla tried to make a Godzilla noise—she'd done it enough times before that they all got it.

"Vodka drinks or cider?" Derrick said, now standing, leaning down into the car.

"Both," Lyla said. "We'll be drinking the whole time, probably."

"Got it," Derrick said, slamming the door in his wake.

—

They hadn't planned far enough ahead. All the campgrounds in a one-hundred-mile radius were booked for the weekend. They'd almost scrapped the plan until Derrick remembered his uncle owned farmland way, way out in the middle of nowhere. The uncle sold the crops standing to other farmers. Fifty years ago, a family had lived on the land, and since then, the house was torn down and nearly every foot of property was made use of. Aside from the little hideaway in the woods. The ground in the flat clearing was mossy and never needed cut. There was a creek. There was a campfire pit. There were several cords of ancient wood, cut and stacked by who knew who. And the biggest and nicest luxury was an outhouse with a proper toilet seat.

It took close to three hours to get there but being away from it all suddenly felt very much worth it. Lyla's Samsung Galaxy A7 was hooked to a portable JBL speaker with a built-in battery that would last them most of the weekend. They were into the goofy tracks of their youth, trying to be drunken and happy. Currently, it was Joe Budden's *Pump It Up* and it had them jumping and drunkenly mumbling along. When it ended, a song before their collective knowledge of adult music began and changed the mood entirely.

The trio sat in the sprawl of their gear and howled to the moon: "*...everybody hurts. Take comfort in your friends...*"

Lyla stopped suddenly after the second verse and looked at her bag. Sissy, drunken and pleasantly melancholy, rocked her head side-to-side while Derrick sang into his Strongbow can.

"My bag moved," Lyla said.

"Sing with us," Sissy said, teary-eyed.

"No, for real. My bag moved." Lyla crawled away from the sleeping bag where they all sat. She picked up the bag—simple brown canvass with leather accents and heavy-duty zippers. She looked inside, keeping her distance, as if there might be a rat hiding out.

"Hmm," she said when there was nothing untoward. Beneath, however, was a smooth, ovular rock. "Was that…?" she trailed before ignoring its existence. "Think I'm drunk."

"I know I am," Sissy said.

"We *all* know you are," Derrick said.

The trio laughed with honest mirth, and in that moment, things were beautiful and perfect. The fire ate through the old wood, and each took regular turns feeding the flames, always from the nearest stacked row. There were three rows and two were beyond where light reached, making them more trouble than worth troubling over.

Sissy returned to the fire with three ant-infested chunks of cedar. Without ceremony, she dropped them into the ashy firepit. Frantic and cringing, she swiped at her hands and arms to be sure she wasn't carting any miniscule stowaways. She sat down next to Derrick. Lyla had her head leaned against his shoulder. The little speaker had been on a somber R&B ride for the last twenty minutes. Nodding along to something old school from Monica, Sissy tipped her can. The warm dregs went down her throat and she grimaced.

"Do I drink another or—?"

A rock crashing into the most distant woodpile silenced her question.

"Tell me that was the wind," Lyla said.

"What wind?" Derrick said. "You grab wood from that pile?"

Sissy shook her head, eyes wide.

"Sounded like a rock hit it," Lyla said, her voice low and warning.

"Way out here?" Derrick said. "Nah, probably we spooked a racoon or something."

"Yeah," Sissy said.

"I guess," Lyla said.

Seconds mounted in silence. Sissy leaned back to pull her cellphone from her jeans pocket. According to the clock, it was 12:01 AM. "I'm pretty tired," she said. "Going to take a pee, then call it. You can stay up if you want to."

Derrick swished his can around some.

"I just cracked this," Lyla said, holding up her can.

"I'll help finish it. Besides, if we drink too much, we'll be dead all tomorrow," Derrick said.

Sissy clicked on the flashlight app on her phone and started across the mossy ground to the gloomy and spider-ridden outhouse. A shudder passed through her at about the halfway point as she moved into the shadows of the looming trees; it felt as if something was looking at her. She accepted it without proof and the best she could do was to modify the animal.

"Just a racoon. They smell campers a million miles away. Like sharks to camper-er-er-ers," she said, the final word coming out in something like comedic terror.

"You say something?" Lyla said.

"No," Sissy said.

The outhouse looked clean inside—she'd inspected it well enough while there was still light—but it was so dark she could no longer trust anything. And yet…she dropped her pants and sat. The vodka drinks and the cider had mingled in her guts and turned the food she'd eaten and digested into a gassy bomb. She wasn't sitting more than a minute before an absolutely bragworthy fart blew out of her. Despite that that little speaker packed some punch, she guessed that they heard her, and she began to laugh.

Sissy shined the cellphone's flash to her left to find the roll of toilet paper Lyla had installed on her first visit. She waited to hear Lyla or Derrick laughing as well, but it didn't happen. However, outside, there were three loud clunks. Derrick shouted something angry and scared sounding. Sissy moved quickly then.

"What the fuck!" Derrick said.

"Sissy!" Lyla said.

"Get in the car!" Derrick said.

An animalistic growl lit the night and made her decompressed guts swirl anew, as if there might be a reason that she could stay in that outhouse forever. She didn't pause however, yanking her pants up and fastening the button as the sounds of glass shattering and voices screaming filled the once agreeable night. She swung open the door hard enough that the hinges creaked and the handle banged against an outside wall.

There were two enormous furry creatures terrorizing Sissy's friends. One had put Derrick through the hatch window of the car and was reeling his stunned and woozy form out. The other pulled at Lyla's ankles, her arms wrapped around the passenger's side rear tire of the car. Her grip slipped and the beast tossed her. She belly-flopped onto the fire and immediately rolled onto their things. She began rooting into her purse as the beast grabbed her anew. The other sasquatch had Derrick propped against the back of the car, feeding from his abdomen like his body was an open buffet.

Sissy was already running toward the action, her legs working on some buried impulse, her arms swinging, her hands open, her phone somewhere in the dewy moss. She grabbed the blade-less hockey stick they'd been using to stir the fire. Its tip glowed red beneath a shelf of ashy gray like a cigarette tip. Derrick was worse off, so her body took her there. She jabbed the stick at the beast, unintentionally slamming the hot, hot tip into the beast's ear canal. It howled and swung backward, nailing Sissy and sending her spinning through the air like a maple pod in a windstorm.

She landed a few feet from Lyla. She had the stun gun pulled from her purse and it was obvious she'd already nailed the beast because it watched her like an uncertain, though still ferocious, junkyard dog. Sissy tried to call out but the crash to the ground had sent the wind from her lungs.

"Come on, you freak!" Lyla said. She was on her feet, waving the weapon with more menace than Sissy had ever seen in her friend.

The sasquatch took a step back and Lyla stepped forward. Sissy tried to call out again as the massive beast that had destroyed Derrick labored by, its movements a touch off-kilter. Blood glistened as it ran down the side of its head.

"Lyla," Sissy said, her voice like the hiss from a popped bicycle tire. "Lye-la."

The laboring sasquatch grabbed Lyla's head from behind and twisted her neck while lifting. Lyla spun around, the taser flying from her grip and landing in the fire. Little green flames began rising from the melting plastics. The beasts knelt over Lyla and tore her apart.

"No," Sissy wailed quietly.

She crawled to the red and black can of Zippo lighter fluid. She kept on crawling, her ribs screaming inside her chest while her left ankle throbbed and dragged in a way that felt too disconnected to be good. She grabbed a flaming chunk of wood and threw it next to the beasts. The little white nozzle was tough enough to get open that she bent her fingernail in half, creasing it.

"Burn," she said and squeezed the 12 ounce can, waving her arm like a sprinkler. The flames leapt and caught upon the beasts, and they popped upright, surprised and obviously scared. Sissy crawled closer. "Eat shit and die," she said, a little more oxygen was now getting to her lungs.

The sasquatches were quickly out of her reach. Sissy refused to take her eyes off them. For hours, after they'd put out the fires from their backs, they stayed on the edge of the campsite. Sissy burned the entire pile closest to the fire—several dozen stove-lengths of wood. The beasts watched her as well, when morning came and the light was plentiful, she found where Derrick's phone had gotten to. She called 911, unaware that the nightmare was far from over.

CHAPTER FOURTEEN
JOHN NOLAN

The gentle breeze pushing nearby tree branches against one another and the crackle of the shrunken flames of the campfire made up all the sounds around the circle. The guests sat silent, reverently so. What they'd just heard wasn't exciting or nice, the way Sissy had told it carried so much of the heartbreak she'd bared that it soured the whole of having a Squatcher-Con at all.

At least for most of them.

John wasn't one of that sub-group. He was counting in his head. Sure, Sissy's story was sad, and it was terrible what had happened, a complete tragedy, but he'd been working on this experiment for months. He'd been obsessing over sasquatch so much of his life. He'd finally done something no one else had been able to do since the beginning of recorded time.

What the others didn't know was that John's aunt owned the hotel and lodge property. She had seen things and had shown John things. She was the reason John had gotten into squatching in his youth. They'd been different, way back when, more like a team. But she wasn't doing so well lately. The best she could do now was offer him use of the property, a bit of cash, a connection or two, and all the spirit she could psychically transmit from indoors.

In fact, it was she who had come up with the plan to catch the local sasquatch they knew to live in the forest next to the lodge. It was she who had a friend who worked at a funeral home—a man whose son had done very wicked things in a rented room and had had the benefit of a manager willing to cover up the discretions in exchange for future favors. The undertaker friend had cut thirty-nine holes in the backs of thirty-nine recently deceased skulls to remove their brains—brains being a sasquatch delicacy recently noted in incidents from around the globe. It had been she who funded the massive cage. It had been she who put together the light systems and tripwires. It had been she who had removed any shred of doubt as to the existence of the cryptid. It had been she who had arranged things so that John could stand face-to-face with a living, breathing sasquatch.

He'd be rich. He'd be famous. The entire world would know the name John Nolan.

"Can I have another beer?" Sissy said, her words slurring some.

John was grateful for the break in silence. He pushed to his feet and stepped to the cooler. "Anyone else want one? We're going for a short walk. My story isn't quite a story, more like a visual offering."

There were no arguments. Everyone stood, aside

from Sissy.

"Can I stay behind?" she said.

John frowned. It wasn't always easy to remember to be empathetic to people in the face of greatness. "I suppose it'll be all right. You've fulfilled your part. The rest of you, you'll want to see what I have to show you. I promise you."

"Do you have bones?" Freddy said.

"A corpse?" Billy said, eyebrows almost touching the spot where his hairline had been up until his twenty-first birthday.

John grinned, eyes alight. "It's a surprise," he said, then thought, *You will bow down to your king in just fifteen minutes.* "Everyone have what they need for a short walk?"

The guest attractions of Squatcher-Con 2022 took turns looking at each other before glancing at the broken shell of what had become Sissy.

"Maybe I ought to stay behind with Sissy," Amy said.

John clenched his teeth. "We won't be long, and you of all people need to see this."

"Why me of all people?" Amy said.

John took three deep breaths, calming himself. "Just…just follow me, okay? I paid for you to be here, please. Just follow me. We won't be long."

"I need to be alone a minute," Sissy said.

"Perfect. Now, let's get moving," John said and pulled a flashlight from his jacket pocket. He clicked it on. He began walking toward a hiking trail that would act as a cross-country skiing route during the winter months. From behind him, a pair of flashlights clicked to life and a cellphone shined a blue, blue halo onto the overgrown grass between the high fir trees and the path where they walked.

None of them really needed those lights. John didn't need to tell them either. He'd show them. Showing was infinitely better than telling; ask anyone who ever demanded proof. Through a thick patch of trees, limbs brushing against passerby shoulders, the forest began to thin. Ahead, a boxy building loomed in a perfect blanket of shadow. John quickened his pace. His flashlight beam fell onto a fat, ABUS padlock. The flashlight fit snugly beneath his armpit as he withdrew a keyring from his pants pocket.

"What's this?" Billy said.

"Patience," John said. He opened the door and shined his beam onto the secondary power panel. He threw three switches. Stadium-like lighting began to hum as it warmed. The darkness wasn't exactly cut yet but was thinning. "Takes about three minutes before they're all the way live."

"How far do they go?" Nancy said.

"Another three-quarter mile," John said. He started along the trail again. "Come on."

As they walked, the forest sounds grew louder and louder until it was obvious that they were unnatural, being piped in. John wondered if any of them might guess why. None asked. He glanced back. Billy was directly behind him and wore a quizzical expression.

John thought, *All will be revealed soon.*

A little ways ahead, the trees thickened again and despite the big lights coming alive, it was impossible to see through. John grinned wider now. This kind of tree didn't grow this thickly together, not naturally.

"Hey, what the hell is this?" Billy said, almost

having to yell to be heard over the piped in nature sounds. He clicked on his flashlight and pointed it at what appeared to be a solid wall of trees.

"Part of what I have to show you." John stopped and turned a few feet short of the tree wall. "I'm sorry about the noise, but it had to be done to get a leg up on the…game."

"What game?" Amy said.

"What's behind the wall?" Nancy said.

"You didn't?" Freddy said.

Billy gulped, and his face blanched. "You have one? Do you really have one?"

"Before I show you, I need to see you all power down your cellphones," John said.

Freddy and Billy couldn't shut down their phones fast enough. Waving the closing screens like air traffic controllers.

"I just have a pay-as-you-go flip phone," Sydney said as he pulled it from his pocket. "Battery lasts about three weeks at the rate I use it." He powered down as well.

Nancy pulled out her phone and looked at the screen. "Why?" she said.

"Rules. Trust me here, okay?" John said.

"What about airplane mode?" Amy said.

"Shut down the fucking phones!" John said, frantic, smiling maniacally.

Nancy did, but Amy didn't.

"What if I don't want to?" she said.

John stiffened. "Then nobody sees the actual ninth fucking wonder of the world!"

"Turn off that phone, or so help me I will turn it off for you," Billy said, and Freddy nodded to this.

"Whoa, I was only asking." Amy held down the power button and then tapped the red logo that appeared on the screen. "See. It's powered down."

"Thank you," John said. The lights overhead were fully warmed and he now had no trouble seeing what he was doing as he fiddled with the panel that hid another heavy padlock. A section of forest wall eased open a few inches. "Prepare to see what you might've thought mythical. Prepare to know there is more to this world. Prepare to understand what I have done for all of you. You before all else in the entire world."

John pulled open the door and stepped through.

CHAPTER FIFTEEN
AMY SNELL

To the left of the doorway she'd stepped through was a big, brown speaker hanging from a tree. It had her undivided interest for about two seconds before she heard rustling and let her eyes wander deeper into the brightly lit knoll that had been hidden behind the wall of false trees. A ten-by-ten cage of heavy iron bars sat in the grass. It had to be about eight feet tall, and the beast within was crouched, seething out at the humans. Amy went no closer even as all the others did.

"I can't believe it," Freddy said.

"It's beautiful," Billy said. "How?"

Amy began mapping the space, the same way she did whenever she went home from a bar with a stranger. Potential exit points were important to know. It appeared there might be several. From the inside of the pen John had created, and with the lights on, the fake forest wall was clear and the many doorframes were visible. Though, so were some locks.

It almost felt as if she was standing on the set of a

science-fiction movie. The way John did things, she knew if she looked around hard enough, she'd find cameras. He'd probably sell it someday, maybe put it in the bonus features of his autobiography. It wasn't a wonder they'd had to power down their cellphones.

"My mother and aunt, my grandparents, for as long as I can remember, they'd told tales of this forest and the sasquatch who lived here. As for this setup, my aunt and I were comparing notes on things we'd heard from around the world. All the recent stories and all the old ones coming to light thanks to the internet," John said.

The beast was looking at each human face as if trying to save it to memory. It stopped on Amy and stared. She felt it deeply, like the lustful male gaze, like in high school when the quarterback started to take notice of the once shy girl turned budding woman, like the men at last call at every bar on the face of the planet. That depth of desire was all that held anything close to similarity. Though this look was piercing and cold and deadly. This was menace incarnate, and Amy had no doubt that this monster wanted to devour her. Wanted to peel her skull like a banana skin and suck out the meat of her brain.

"She's wealthy and has the perfect spot, so we used my knowledge and her elements. First came the speakers and the lighting." John pointed to a light and then to one of the speakers. "Once those were in place, my aunt hired a cement crew to come out and labor—it's the off-season for most cement jobs, so they were happy for the work. They lugged the cell bars out. They were welded and wired by yet another small team—all happy for the work. They hoisted it high and set the snare trap."

Amy broke the stare-down with the sasquatch to see the pulleys and ropes hanging from what appeared to be fake ancient spruce trees. Well-done fakes at that. This was all too much to not be something Hollywood adjacent. Though she believed all that she saw, she forced a sense of logic to overshadow all else. On shaky legs, she started toward the cage.

"Laborers then helped build these tall walls that surround the pen here." John again pointed out what was clearly visible. It was as if he'd planned this entire speech. "We then hired ten—well fifteen, originally—student artists from the college in town. It was tough at first. I had to fire five of them for demanding they be given artistic license to give their take on what this forest would look like. You could tell none of those ones had ever had to pay their own way; didn't know that sometimes making art was no different from standing on an assembly line."

Amy stepped up behind Nancy, who was nodding at John's comparison. Amy ran it back in her head and for a moment, forgot the beast and decided John Nolan could be fairly astute. It was entirely possible to race through multiple renditions of a piece of art and have them all come out worthwhile, all come out rewarding. This was the kind of lesson artists learned after years of struggle—the kind of lesson that let her look back on all the bit roles and bad movies she'd been in with fresh eyes.

The sasquatch growled, bringing her from her thoughts. Amy continued moving closer, passing Nancy and Sydney, who'd both remained a solid fifteen feet from the cage.

"Good art and sounds and a sturdy trap, that's not nearly enough. This is where my aunt's foresight really came into play." John tapped his temple as he delivered the sermon. "Smart, smart woman. I won't go too much into details, but she has a record of a young man doing a very, very bad thing, and this young man's father just happens to be a mortician."

Amy was now only six feet away and moving beyond the animated John Nolan. He was like a revival preacher right then, but he almost had to be. The speakers weren't pointed directly into the pen, but they were still quite loud.

"Brains. You used brains, didn't you?" Billy said, jerking around to look over his shoulder where he stood about three feet from the cage, just out of reach should the sasquatch decide to try for a handful of human.

"That's right," John said, grin faltering some at Billy stealing a smidge of shine from his polished presentation. "Brains. For months, I've gone out into the woods and dropped a few brains a week. The first ones were miles out, and I tell you, I made good use of my GPS device."

Freddy laughed gently.

"Did you ever see *King Kong?*" Sydney asked, his voice full of awe.

Billy spun around. "Sasquatch is no ape," he said, sneering, eyes brimming with hatred.

Amy had kept on moving closer, was now side-by-side, and then passing Freddy and Billy. She stopped two feet from the cage. The sasquatch scent permeated like a corpse flower in bloom. Amy had to swallow a rising wetness in her mouth as the sweat of pre-sickness crept into her system, warning her that she would soon vomit if an element was not changed.

"Amy?" Nancy said.

The sasquatch was again making hard eye-contact with Amy, and she heard nothing any of them said around her.

"I'd step back," Freddy said.

"Too close, don't get so close," Billy said.

"Amy!" Nancy said again.

Amy snapped to and turned her head. At that moment, the sasquatch jerked an arm between bars. Its nails took a few shreds of her jacket but no more as Billy had pulled her away just in time.

Amy looked at her jacket and then the claws of the beast. What had been torn away remained dangling like candle wax. God, it was terrifying. She had her proof, the very proof needed to squash that hopeful logic she'd harbored. She began walking backwards.

John continued, as if he hadn't been interrupted. "It was only a matter of time and patience to draw this sasquatch closer and closer. I'd actually begun to consider moving the date of this year's Squatcher-Con, but decided since I was able to land Sissy White, she would be a good enough plan B, and then next year have this glorious specimen."

Amy was backing away much quicker than her pace of approach. Nancy reached for her, though didn't fight when Amy kept moving, eyes hard on the cage. The sasquatch had seemingly lost interest in her and was focused on Nancy. She didn't trust the shift in attention, knowing it wanted her. Wanted to feast upon her flesh and wash it down with her spilled blood.

What am I doing out here? she thought.

"You wouldn't believe it, but it's as if this sasquatch knew it had a scheduled appearance and wandered into the trap about twenty-one hours ago. My aunt spent the entire day out here; it had her so excited she had to go to bed right after supper."

Amy bumped into the wall and finally let her eyes lead her. She felt detached from her body, as if a puppet master pulled levers inside her brain...and that monster, it ate brains. *God!* This was a nightmare.

"This bad for me, how bad will it be for Sissy?" she whispered, barely hearing her voice over the raucous forest sounds being pumped from the speakers to overshadow anything human. The setup really was ingenious. She stepped through the door. And with every step away from the knoll and the cage, the path grew dimmer, and those overloud sounds dissipated. "Bad, bad, bad, that's how it'll be," she said, finishing her thought.

She was thinking far ahead, of leaving and making do with the other cons in the future, the ones where she was less of a celebrity, but the only thing she had to worry about was the check clearing. She was thinking so far ahead that she didn't see what was on the trail before her, hidden behind the fresh shadow where the high lights did not touch. She reached into her pocket for her cellphone. It awoke, though was taking an irritatingly long time. All she wanted was to use the flashlight app, then maybe the phone to call a cab and get the hell out of this horror. Once it was possible, she began flicking through the pages of apps. Everything melded together on her screen and nothing was what she wanted.

She smelled it but didn't acknowledge the smell in time.

Enormous matching hands came down on her shoulders, instantly snapping both clavicles like they were dry twigs. She screamed, dropping her cellphone into the grass at her feet.

Moonlight shined enough to reflect dull wetness from the beast's eyes. Amy opened her mouth to scream again, but the sasquatch planted a kiss on her and began shredding her cheeks and lips and tongue with its tremendous teeth; chewing through her like she was blueberries and crust in a pie-eating contest at the county fair. Blood gushed and her knees turned to rubber. The sasquatch swung her off the path and leaned her against the tree, like they were passionately necking.

It only slowed to swallow. In less than a minute, the sasquatch had eaten Amy's face beneath her nose. It let her drop in order to chew what it had in its mouth, crunching through jaw and teeth before kneeling over the barely alive body.

Amy's mind tried to rally her limbs until the very moment before whatever was inside her brain that made her who she was, slipped free. In that moment was acceptance and relaxation. She'd never have to pander to greasy, stinky man-boys who carted around topless stills of her, demanding they be signed. She'd never have to sleep in a cheap motel room or the back of a rental car. She'd no longer exist as a starving C-grade actor.

The sasquatch feasted. It took its time, luxuriating in the delicious hot meats of the once Amy Snell.

CHAPTER SIXTEEN
SYDNEY FROMM

Sydney Fromm was amazed, but the amazement waned quickly, or rather, shifted. He'd always been open-minded about most things—aside from omnipotent gods, he'd gotten over that once he was old enough to think for himself, despite the indoctrination he'd received as a youth. The setup John had done to catch this thing, now that was kind of amazing.

For weeks lately, his mind had been elsewhere. The biggest chunk being on the most recently completed novel saved to his computer's hard drive. He needed to get it to the editor, but his lead had some flaws, or at least, potential flaws. An actor in B-genre flicks, he had an idea about the lifestyle, as it seemed an actor loved nothing more than talking about themselves, but it was missing something real and textured. A small part of why he'd agreed to come was because he wanted to pick Amy Snell's brain, borrow a few gritty realities from the hard road to Hollywood and all the dirty alleyways it took you. Everybody knew about the glamorous and the exceptionally horrible, but what about the spaces between?

"What are you going to do with it after the weekend?" Nancy said.

"It is my duty to make the sasquatch available to scientific research. It would simply be an act of pure selfishness and shortsightedness to keep this amazing creature from the public. Who knows what can be gained from my achievement?" John said.

Amy had left maybe three minutes ago, and right now seemed like his chance to get her alone and mine for some gold. Without a word, Sydney turned from the show and John's endless, self-congratulatory speech, and exited the pen. Though the nature sounds remained loud, being those extra feet away from the conversation concerning the sasquatch felt like the calm after a storm. And with every step, the noise coming from the speakers became less ominous.

Ahead, he saw where the shadow ate the final remnants of light shined down from the overhead lamps. Sydney withdrew his phone and booted it up. He got an idea then and searched out Amy's website—he'd bluffed a little, though it was a flip phone, it was newish and could surf the internet in a rudimentary fashion. Suggesting abstinence from new tech was part of his schtick. She had an email listed in her bio—for business enquiries only. He clicked it twice and his email account opened. Quickly, he shot off a short note, asking her if he could ply her with liquor from the bar in exchange for some war stories from the path to the big screen. He then promised that this was not a come on.

Two seconds passed before he heard a ping and a short-lived flash of light from the trees ahead. He took two steps and stopped to locate his flashlight app.

"Amy?" he said.

The light shined a blue swatch deep enough into the trees to give Sydney at least a second's head start when he saw those obsidian eyes, that massive head, and that fur, sopping dark, dark red. He made use of that second, sprinting back toward the pen and the others.

John hadn't said a word about any additional beasts, so he obviously didn't know. Sydney got to wondering if they were like rats: was this forest teeming with them? Maybe, unlikely, but maybe.

"Hey!" he shouted, despite knowing nobody would hear him until he reached the door. And, boy, when he reached that door, he was going to slam it closed behind him.

Grass rustled. A deep groan panted nearer.

Sydney dared a glance back. Turned out the sasquatch was significantly faster than he was. A giant, furry palm slammed across the side of his head, sending him pinwheeling and bursting his eardrum. Momentum put him against a tree. He leaned there like a punch-drunk boxer, his vision swimming, but he climbed to his feet.

With no direction in mind, he bolted into the darkness. After ten steps, he nailed another tree. He pushed upright again and was suddenly facing light. Light was good. He ran hard, hard, hard. Something slammed into him from below the chin and sent him straight down, whiplashing him. All the breath left his lungs and he looked up at a quadruple-visioned sasquatch. It dripped blood on to his face.

"Help," he said, meekly.

The sasquatch dropped its knees, landing on either side of Sydney's hips. It leaned over him as if studying an apple, figuring the just right spot to bite.

"Please."

The sasquatch bent closer, its scent full and awful, but in one way familiar. As a teen, Sydney had an afterschool job at a county butcher shop. A massive place with more than twenty men and women on staff. On Saturday mornings, he was often there before the others to make deliveries. The meat came straight from the abattoir, the pink paper packs still warm to the touch. The scent of blood full and thick. Almost as thick as right now.

"Please," he said again.

In a vampiric gesture, the sasquatch tipped its head and struck for Sydney's neck. Much more than a pair of overlong eyeteeth punctured his jugular. Both rows with the beast's jaw bit down hard enough to end Sydney Fromm's life in a flash.

A courtesy really, not that a sasquatch could think about such things. It chewed and drank, then paused. It reached out an index finger with a great claw and scratched through the flesh, muscle, and bone. The sasquatch yanked him up against its chest and finished cutting around the back of Sydney's skull. His brainpan came away with a wet pop. The sasquatch tossed the unwanted morsel and sucked the brain out of his skull before chewing gently, head slightly upturned to the moon. It dropped Sydney's body and stood there a few moments, basking in the view from flavor country.

CHAPTER SEVENTEEN
SISSY WHITE

Sissy's jacket sleeves were damp with snot and tears. After the others left, the emotions plowed through her. She remembered her friends as they'd been. Speaking it aloud brought everything back anew and a couple beers and a little hard liquor did not help her. Lyla had been her friend since second grade. In tenth grade, Derrick finally, finally made his move and asked Lyla to a date at the bowling alley. That new relationship had changed almost nothing about Sissy's relationship with Lyla. Most times, the three of them hung out, and occasionally, Sissy would have a date and they'd made it a foursome.

A smile crept to Sissy's lips when she remembered the limo to prom. She'd been hard up for a date and accepted an offer from Dale Roberts, a second-string basketball player with big hands and an even bigger forehead. They'd stopped in front of Dale's house and she and Lyla could both tell Derrick was nervous. Though he'd grown out of being the easiest target, there'd been years of abuse. The usual stuff. Twice janitors had had to come along to let him out of lockers. Once a student dishwasher from a Chinese buffet had to let him out of a dumpster. Numerous times in the gym locker room, the football and basketball players from his class took him by the arm and made simple contact: his hand to their penises.

Dale climbed into the limo and looked at Derrick, only nodding. They started taking shots of Smirnoff with Miller Genuine Draft chasers. After the third, Dale asked Derrick if he was wearing Brute: "Is that Brute?" he repeated, face in a sneer. Derrick had cringed and said it was, and that he'd borrowed it from his dad. "That's dick-toucher cologne," Dale had said and lightning fast, like a gunslinger, Lyla pulled the taser her mother had bought her from her purse and slammed it into Dale's neck. He instantly shit his pants, uncertain of exactly what had happened. They berated him until he climbed out of the limo and walked home. For years they'd made jokes: *I almost Daled myself* or *Better take the dog for a walk, he needs to Dale.*

To Sissy's knowledge, Lyla only used that taser one other time, and it hadn't worked even half as well on a sasquatch as it had on a lonely dweeb trying to make the abuse he'd taken run downhill to the next loser.

"Fuck," she hissed and slammed back the remainder of her third solo can of beer.

The cooler was down to soda and water, so she left the barely burning campfire and made for the side door into the hotel. It was locked.

"Ugh."

She followed pink patio stones around to the front of the building. The light there was mellow and welcoming, but the doors were locked there as well. Everything was nice enough, though dated. There was nowhere for her to tap her room card. She tried the doorbell button and waited and waited. She tried it again. Minutes began mounting as she stared at the uneventful apps on her phone.

She couldn't stand out here all night. She returned to the campfire and considered tossing in another log. No. She would go get John and make him come back with her to open the damned door. She again pushed to her feet. She was drunk but handling it well enough to keep from wobbling. She didn't bother using her flashlight app until she made it into deep forest. Far ahead, bright lights lit the path and she needed that; the damned flashlight app ate battery like no other.

At least she wasn't sad anymore, only pissed at John and his aunt. Who locked the doors without an attendant when guests were staying? It was a goddamned con, didn't they hire extra staff? Did nobody actually come to this thing?

CHAPTER EIGHTEEN
NANCY HARGENSON

The men were talking shop and Nancy couldn't bring herself to care much, not in the face of such a revelation. The way the sasquatch's eyes followed her was eerie; it seemed almost as if the thing had a secret, a little nugget of wisdom that it would spring on them. She'd step left, then right and its eyes remained pinned on her. She moved around steadily, subtly so the men wouldn't notice…until a moment after something struck the back of her foot. The beast looked down. She trailed the sasquatch's gaze to the strange pink bowl. Little blue lines within its concave inner streaked decorative lightning bolts around the surface. The bowl appeared to have hair on the underside.

She looked back to the doorway, to where it must've come from, and saw nothing. She knelt and picked up the bowl. It was hot to the touch, and softer than she expected. It smelled like metal but was not metal. She did her best to avoid touching the pink stuff and studied what she assumed was the bottom. That was definitely hair. Real hair…human hair.

Then she got it.

"No," she gasped and tossed the cranium to the ground and began backing away while absently wiping her palms on her pants.

The men took no notice of her. She bypassed the cage and kept moving in reverse until striking a far wall with her shoulders. She jumped then and turned. There was a door a few steps to her left. She found the slat that lifted—there was a matching slat on the far side, which allowed the lock to be accessed while inside or outside. She yanked on it. It wouldn't budge.

"John! Let me out!"

John faced her, frowning. "The open door's just back there. Where we came in."

"Look!" Nancy pointed to the ground where she'd tossed the top of Sydney's head.

In the cage, the sasquatch began making noises: a mix of hooting and growling. Like a bear and like a gorilla, as if this thing might be where the genetics of the two species forked off into new directions however many thousands of years ago.

John first focused on the beast and then to the ground. It took him a moment to find the cranium. The sasquatch started to pound its great fists against the forest floor. Billy and Freddy were entranced by the action.

"Look!" Nancy shouted again as she tugged on the padlock.

John finally saw enough to step back, away from the door, away from the cage, away from Freddy and Billy. The sasquatch began howling wolfishly, showing yet another side. John faced it as he stumbled, going nowhere.

"No! Look!" Nancy said, almost jumping with anxious energy.

John understood then that she didn't mean the cranium or the sasquatch, but the door. Peering inside, as if taking in a dinner menu, was another sasquatch. John sprinted to Nancy, not a word of warning to the pair watching the raging sasquatch within its cell.

"Hurry!" Nancy said.

The second sasquatch stepped into the knoll in a way that was far too knowing. It was creeping, and so, so humanistic in its movements. How long had it watched John and his aunt? How smart was it? Did it pick up things? The beast looked high above the dropped cell and followed steel cables that fed into an electronic box.

John reached into his pocket and pulled out his keys. His hands shook. The keys fell into the grass at his feet. He squealed childishly.

"Come on, dammit!" Nancy said.

"What are you doing?" Billy said, still about three feet from the cell.

The second sasquatch began palming at the electrical box. It had to have been out here before its mate had been caught, had to have watched John test the mechanics. Now, it was mimicking the simple act of button-pushing. Nancy shook her head. These self-titled experts knew nothing about this creature. What if they were smarter than apes? Its movements and expressions were so unbearably human, so full of layered thoughts and considerations.

"Hurry the fuck up!" Nancy said.

The second sasquatch started using its middle finger to prod the electrical box. John finally located the correct key and inserted it into the heavy padlock. At that same moment, the cell began rising as the wenches reeled-in the cables.

Freddy stood dumbly, staring at the soon to be freed beast while Billy looked around before breaking for the door they'd come through. The second sasquatch launched itself from the electrical box, taking in eight feet per stride. Once close enough, it leapt at Billy, slamming his hip against the doorframe. The breaking of bones snapped out like a lash while the rest of him whipped around, rubbery against the unmoving frame. He screamed as the sasquatch rolled his upper half—his bottom half hardly moved, as it remained tethered only by fleshy tissue. In a flash, the beast brought down a clawed hand, slamming through skin and bone and everything in-between, stopping for less than a second before reefing free Billy's still-beating heart, blood oozing down the pelt of its forearm.

In that singular moment, Billy's eyes got big and then all the muscles in his body relaxed.

In the middle of the pen, Freddy was shaking. The sasquatch that had been in the cell stood straight and took two human-sized steps toward him. He swallowed.

"I love you," he said.

Somewhat gingerly, the sasquatch put its great hands on either side of Freddy's face. Freddy licked his lips as tears ran down his cheeks.

"I love you."

The sasquatch stretched its thumbs straight.

"I love—ah!"

Those thumbs bent and the clawed nails entered Freddy's eyeholes. Blood replaced the tears, cascading red, red rivers over his flesh, painting his chest and bulbous belly with gore. The sasquatch lifted its thumbs, increasing the flow down his face, making it chunky and multi-colored: greens and whites added to Death's rainbow. A great creaking snap rang out and the cranium popped off. The beast let the body fall and went after the juicy brain that had jumped free at the pressure and now slipped along the grass.

A hand yanked Nancy back and she screamed. But it was John, pulling her from the pen. He closed the door. Heavy footfalls raced in their direction. John moaned, fumbling with the key still in the lock, but managed to clamp it and withdraw the key. It was only a second after that that one of the sasquatches began slamming against the far side of the door.

"Run," John said.

Nancy let him lead. They chased into the blackness of the thick forest.

CHAPTER NINETEEN
SISSY WHITE

The sensation of danger oozed from the deep forest shadows. The realization that she hadn't been in a forest since that fateful night stopped her dead. She closed her eyes, weighing what to do. Lyla's face flashed before her, those pleading eyes and the piercing screams.

It was an evolutionary hanger-on, fear of the dark, and despite knowing this, her mind jumped for terror. Anything could be out there in those shadows: coyotes, wolves…sasquatches.

Sissy turned around and took nine hurried steps back toward the lodge but stopped again. No, she had to conquer this. This illogic would not rule her. She would not sit alone by a fading campfire until who knew when. She was a capable and mindful adult. This was the modern world and too close to civilization for monsters, surely.

She switched direction again. Into the darkness, slowly chasing down that semi-distant light. On shaky legs, she walked. The terror mounted and pinged an inner sensor: this wasn't simple illogic. She knew something was wrong. She saw only trees and shadows. She heard only regular forest night sounds. But she understood on a level below the surface, something was awaiting her.

"Don't be stupid."

Behind her, a branch snapped. She broke into a run, certain a sasquatch chased close behind her. Somehow it would sense that she'd escaped the furry claws of Death once before, it would smell it on her. Payback time was inevitable.

"Stop. Being. Crazy," she said as she crossed the last of the shadow and entered the warm glow of the lights that had been strung up in the trees. She slowed and drank in the scene. "Why would someone light the forest? Why did they come out here?"

The word experiment flashed on her mind. *Hadn't John said experiment?*

Experimenting with what?

She carried forward, her eyes trying to make sense of what appeared to be a wall of phony trees. And likely she only recognized that much because someone had splashed glistening red paint. The out-of-place-ness of the colorful strikes did not fit with the fine mimicry of the trees on the wall. She squinted, trying to understand as she drew closer.

What insane thing had John Nolan prepared for Squatcher-Con 2022?

CHAPTER TWENTY
JOHN NOLAN

John and Nancy had made it about twenty yards into the dark forest beyond the pen, which happened to be a scary distance from the resort's lodge while giant beasts were loose and on the prowl. John pulled Nancy to a stop next to a very old spruce tree. Both were panting and red-faced, the color visible even in the shadowy forest.

Through gasped breaths, John said, "We need to split up and wind back around. If we stay together, we're both toast."

"That's insane. If they catch us one at a time—"

"If they catch us at all, we're done. We split up. It gives each of us a chance and perhaps it confuses the sasquatches long enough for us to get to safety."

Nancy shook her head with emphatic swings. "That's crazy. I don't want to die alone out here!" She pulled her cellphone out of her pocket and powered it up. The red circle with a slash and the

AT&T logo with its five rising bars next to it swapped off and on. The service was shaky but there, somewhere out here she'd get a good, strong signal. "Are you getting service?"

"Shh! No time for that. Now, you go that way and I go this way. Good luck."

Nancy straightened from the tree. "Fuck you, I hope you die out here."

John didn't wait for her to leave before he started away. The hope was that the sasquatches would smell her rather than him, or at least prefer the smell of her to him. He'd taken steps in case something had happened: he'd eaten vegetables, faked drinking the soda from his can, wore pine-scented deodorant, and stood over the smoky fire as often as seemed reasonable—though he never really thought it would go down this way. He would've prepared even more, still…what he knew and she didn't was that all the lighting, sound, and auxiliary electrical functions of the sasquatch trap were controlled from a squat but sturdy control room out here in the forest. All he had to do was to get to the control room, call for emergency services, and bask in the luxury and security that cinderblock walls and a heavy door offered.

The trek wasn't straight and that left him guessing where the trail should pick up. He broke branches and crunched through dried forest debris. Silence would've been nice, though in the here and now, speed was the prime point. The sasquatches would hear him even if he thought he was being quiet. This was their world after all.

Behind him, a good distance away it seemed, a

feminine wail echoed through the woods. He grinned. The sasquatches had followed Nancy, surely, and he was all but home free. He pushed through a wall of heavy pine branches and discovered the path. He pumped both fists in a short celebratory jerk before his chest.

"Yes."

His pantlegs were dew damp from the grass and his feet sloshed in their shoes. Step one was to reach the control room. Step two was to call for help with the trusty landline. Step three was to slip out of his socks and put the kettle on. Step four was to act deeply distraught over what had happened. He had video evidence of the beast's existence, so even without the physical proof, he could show and tell his incredible, fame-worthy discovery. The plan was foolproof, so long as he made it.

He shot a glance over his shoulder. The moonlight shined down, mostly unobstructed, along the path. Despite feeling safe, John broke into a jog. Again, far away, someone screamed. If Nancy had made it that long, she'd done better than the others—aside from Sissy who had wisely stayed behind.

CHAPTER TWENTY-ONE
SISSY WHITE

Sissy reached the strange, open doorway into the pen. She gasped mightily through her nose and exhaled an even mightier scream upon seeing the blood. She stumbled forward, into the well-groomed space. She'd been right all along, the time had come, and the sasquatches wanted her. Somehow, they were psychically linked and were having a good old conversation at great distances about finally finishing her off. They'd marked her, or rather, her survival had marked her.

By the time she understood that she was in a pen, she saw the doors, including the open one on the far side. Still, she didn't move toward it. It struck her then how rare it was that anyone believed her about the sasquatch attack. And those who did believe, let their eyes fall glossy with disinterest when she explained that she thought they were smart, that she knew they were killers, and that anybody could fall prey to their savagery. And it wasn't just smart like a pig or a dolphin, they were only a few notches beneath humanity smart.

Right there, standing a few feet from the landing point of the cage dangling overhead, she imagined an escaped lion that was almost as smart as a human.

"No. This isn't that," she said, though she knew it was. "This is a grizzly bear."

She then got to looking at the pen anew. It looked fortress sturdy—not that she had any expertise—so, if she locked herself in, nothing could get at her. But then what?

"Stupid."

In a jog, she doubled-back to the bloody door she'd come through. She found the slat that hid the hasp, understood immediately that somewhere was a padlock to fit the space. But where?

She scanned the bloody grass, now spotting bits of bone and gristle. Somewhere, saved for later, perhaps in a tree or buried under pine needles, was someone's corpse. How many corpses? Was she the last one, again?

"No," she said, this time to the possibility that she was cursed to be the last one left.

There, eight feet to her right, the silver hook of the bulky padlock shined beneath the overhead lights where it lay in a puddle of muddy blood. She hardly considered the blood until it was on her hands, and then only on a minor level—sticky and cool—because the lock was so heavy it had to be good. She closed the door and secured the lock. She pressed against it, trying to force it. Maybe two centimeters of give was an acceptable margin of movement. She dropped her arm, leaving behind a bloody handprint, proof for the eventual investigation that she'd been here, and that people had died violently.

"Maybe only one...maybe that's animal blood," she said, barely above a whisper.

She then hurried across the pen and reached the far door and felt a moment of hope at the lack of blood. She pushed it closed and looked for the padlock. She ran two ovals with her eyes on the ground. Nothing. A huff left her chest. She refused to let herself pause and swung open the door. She stepped out, and there it was, maybe five yards away.

It was in her hands in seconds—oh, that beautiful, heavy lock. Her sneakers slipped on the dewy grass, but she remained upright as she headed back to the door. She was close enough to reach out and touch it when she heard the nearby scream after the crashing of tree limbs. Still, her hands got busy with the slat. Nancy or Amy, she didn't know which. As it had before, that selfless, almost suicidal instinct kicked in and chased after the sound—and if she saw, she didn't store the fact that the hasp within the door had been broken.

Outside, at the edge of the pen, under the bright lights, she had no trouble seeing Nancy beneath a big, nasty sasquatch. The terror and sadness drained away and she became Captain Ahab, demanding revenge over the natural actions of a beast.

"Fuck yooooou!" she screamed as she ran, arcing the ABUS lock over her shoulder and bringing it down the moment the sasquatch looked up. The crunch was much louder than the nature sounds still pumping from the speakers. "Fuck you!" She slammed her foot against the cracked skull a moment after the beast brought its hands up to cradle the wound, as well as to hold its eyeball in place.

The beast rolled to the side, moaning and jerking in pain. Nancy was unconscious. Sissy grabbed her under the armpits and ran backwards. The woman was about 18 pounds lighter than she had been this morning. The sasquatch had broken and then detached her left leg at about mid-thigh. The blood gushed from the wound and Sissy wondered if she did manage to get them to safety, was Nancy going to make it?

The beast was out of view, but its motions were audible through the thick brush.

"Damn, damn," Sissy said as she reached the door of the pen. She didn't have the lock, she'd used it to batter the beast and…the image of the busted hasp flashed on her mind. "Damn!" Once inside, she pushed closed the door and continued dragging Nancy.

She wasn't even a quarter of the way across when the door shook. She got another step, still dragging this woman, this stranger, when wood rubbed against wood—the hideaway slat on the far side of the door being lifted. Sissy got another step and stopped when her heart seemed to stop as well in pure, unhindered terror. The door swung open.

CHAPTER TWENTY-TWO
JOHN NOLAN

It was so dark off the path that John nearly ran past the camouflaged control building. A great weight slipped from his shoulders as he withdrew his keyring and unlocked the door—his hands now steady with confidence. The lights lit automatically. Around him were a computer, two monitors, a basic telephone, rows of circuit breakers with blinking lights, a leather office chair, and a fridge with an electric kettle sat on top. John kicked the door closed behind him. He snatched up the phone and dialed 911.

"Chamberlain nine-one-one, what's the location of your emergency?" a woman said. She was calm and clear.

"Hi, uh, up the ski trail behind Chamberlain Mountain Resort," John said as he bent to retrieve a bottle of water from the floor next to the fridge.

"Oh. We had a call from there not two minutes ago. There's really a situation? The previous caller had hung up after saying she was being chased by a sasquatch." Much of the crispy professionalism had left the woman's voice.

"That's crazy, but some of the people in the group were drinking."

"Do you need police, fire, or EMS?" The woman was once again firm.

"Hmm, EMS with animal control, likely police, too. There's been an animal attack. Multiple dead. Very large bears, perhaps," John said. It hurt to bullshit this part, but he needed this woman to believe him.

"Oh, okay. Are you in a secure place?"

John poured the bottle into the kettle and flipped the switch. "Uh huh. I made it inside."

"And your name, sir?"

"John Nolan. My aunt owns the resort. I'm here with the VIP group that was to head Squatcher-Con."

The woman waited a moment. "Sir, is this sasquatch related?"

"No, that's a coincidence. Though the VIPs...sometimes they're a little obsessed and see bigfoot everywhere. We need help. The bear, maybe bears, have gone wild. They're absolutely savage."

"All right, sir, I've already dispatched police and paramedics. Would you stay on the line until help arrives?"

John fell onto the chair. "Sure, but I don't think they'll find me in the dark. I'm in an electronic control room, not the main lodge or any of the nearby outbuildings." He readied a teabag in a mug. "I guess maybe tell them to come around back of the lodge and follow the trail that leads from the campfire just beyond the rear patio. The campfire might be smoking yet."

"I'm making a note of that. How many are dead and how many are hurt?"

John wondered a moment as he undid his shoes; did he say what he knew or what he figured to be true? "I guess probably four dead or severely injured, at least. One more running around." He then thought again of Sissy who'd lucked out by being screwed in the head.

"Four, you're sure?" The woman was stern.

John slipped his index fingers into the backs of his socks as he pressed the phone to his cheek with his shoulder. "At least." He slipped the socks off and had to bite back a sigh.

"You say at least, from where you are, can you see anyone?"

The kettle clicked and John spun on the chair to fill his cup.

"No. Nothing but bush around me, not that I have a window in here."

From the fridge, John grabbed the Coffee Mate flavored creamer: hazelnut. He put some in the cup and grabbed a pencil from the desk to squeeze the teabag—he didn't much feel like waiting.

"Are you still there, John?"

"Of course. I told you, I'm fine."

The door thumped gently. John looked at it curiously. It was heavy steel, and the walls were cinderblock, he was fine. Just fine. In fact, maybe there'd be one more survivor. He took a breath to mentally ready a bout of display anguish. The doorknob turned. He opened his mouth to feign relief at seeing another human. A sasquatch, fur matted and dripping blood and dirt looked in on him.

"Uh, help!" he said into the phone. "Help, now!"

The sasquatch leapt into the control room and grabbed John, rag-dolling him against the computer and the electrical panels. The nine-one-one operator shouted his name numerous times, but after the first strike, John was hearing nothing. His unconscious body bounced back and forth until everything was smashed and fallen. Bleeding in a puddle of hot tea, John Nolan became the dessert course for a gluttonous beast.

CHAPTER TWENTY-THREE
SISSY WHITE

The one-eyed sasquatch loomed over them, matching Sissy's speed as she backpedaled. It was toying with her. She had no doubt of that. These sonofabitching animals were a menace; did the terror make her meat taste sweet?

It wrinkled its ruined eye and she got it then. She'd made it mad and now it was time for retribution. It felt like she'd been thrown in a gladiator pit as a halftime show. See the beast feast!

A steady whine came up her throat, tears and sweat mingled on her face. She was totally and utterly done, and so was this poor woman being dragged. She stopped then, and let Nancy fall flat. There was nothing she could do to save either of them.

"Come on, then," Sissy said, sniffling back snot and tears.

The beast kept its meandering pace. The stench of the thing bloomed out over the blood scents permeating from all around her. The lights flickered and the beast stilled its forward motion. The pumped-up nature sounds ceased. The lights went out. Quiet reigned for a heartbeat or two before the sound of a chain against a gear unraveled. The whoosh and crash around her were equal parts dull and jarring. In the moonlight, she saw the cell that had been dangling overhead was now over her, as if she'd tripped a snare rather than been the lucky recipient of power failure.

The beast growled. It reached through the bars, swiping at Sissy, but she was several inches beyond touch. Sissy dropped and tried to pull Nancy deeper into the cage. The base had fallen on her whole leg and left her trapped. The sasquatch seemed to see what was happening and adjusted its target. It latched onto Nancy by the front of her jacket. In a rage, it then got to work destroying the woman. Sissy exhaled a heavy breath.

The one positive of Nancy's demise was that she never woke up at any moment while the sasquatch thrashed her head and shoulders against the bars. Sissy closed her eyes. There was no chance that the woman was alive longer than a minute during this beating.

With some of the anger out, the sasquatch got to work on peeling Nancy's cranium. It started slowly, its good eye glistening wetly beneath the moonlight. Sissy couldn't be certain, but it felt like the sasquatch was staring at her as it carved free a consolation prize. It scooped out the brain and slurped it back, taking it like a palmful of Jell-O.

The beast only began to let its focus drift when the distant sounds of sirens filled the sky. It was at this moment that Sissy fully realized she'd probably survive this mess. Would she be blamed? Now she prayed the sasquatch would stay with her long enough for help to arrive, let them see what she saw.

But as a species, the sasquatch had remained hidden because it knew how to read sounds. Sirens were not sounds to play with. With Nancy's entire brain in its mouth, the beast scampered away leaving Sissy alone in the dark—or mostly, she had a corpse and a sturdy cage to keep her company.

CHAPTER TWENTY-FOUR
SISSY WHITE

The interrogation room in the Chamberlain Police Department's station had white walls and a drop tile ceiling, yellowed by the ghosts of cigarettes past. The fluorescent lighting buzzed above her, and the chair wobbled beneath her. It was hot, hot in the room. She'd watched enough cop shows to know this was how they got confessions out of the guilty as well as uncomfortable idiots. She had already been there an hour, long enough to register that they were indeed trying to sweat her, get her to confess to another set of grisly murders. Meaning they totally thought she did it or were so lazy they'd pin this tail on any old donkey within reach.

Turned out she was the only donkey left; everyone had died but her, again.

Nancy's blood was now dry on Sissy's clothes. From a cop point of view, this would likely be pretty damning. The blood of unknown origins on her hands and arms was cracking and flaking: more evidence.

Thank god she'd been locked in a heavy, heavy cage.

Sissy sighed. The booze was wearing off and all she wanted to do was go to bed.

The door opened and a man shaped like Humpty Dumpty stepped in with a pad and pen in his right hand, a cup of coffee in his left. He had a pickle head and was balding down the middle. His eyes were close set and his fingers were disturbingly short.

"Time to spill," he said. "We know you got away with a cockamamie story once, but we here in Chamberlain are from a smarter crop." The detective sat down and slid the pad across the table. "How about you write down just how you did this one, then we'll backtrack and get the first one correct."

Sissy looked at the pad and then at the fish-white belly poking between the gaps of the strained buttons of this idiot cop's shirt. If it wasn't so dire, she might've laughed that this man considered himself smart. After Lyla and Derrick were killed, she'd had to give statements to FBI agents, ones that oozed intelligence and inquiry. This man was nothing but an oaf.

"Is your father a cop?" she said, not taking up the pen.

"Was."

"Makes full sense, knowing that."

"What does?"

"How you'd think you're smarter than anybody. Generational cops are only a step above the Ku Klux Kops who join to kill people of color."

He sneered.

"I mean, you think I tore Nancy Hargenson's leg off and then dragged her to that weird pen, before then dropping a cage on us and slamming her to death. Then I cut off the top of her head, right? With my bare hands?"

The detective sat further back, resting his coffee mug on the crest of his gut. "Yep. You're cold-blooded as I've ever seen. Now, how about we stop rooting around in the mud like a couple a hogs and get to the bacon of the matter."

Sissy closed her eyes and shook her head gently. "What does that even mean?"

"Means, Missy, you're in a world—"

"It's Sissy, dumbass."

The detective clucked his tongue. "Judges 'round here take into account difficult women and their unbecoming attitudes. Not really a crime, but it makes deciding to go heavy on a sentence a little simpler. Not that you'll skate on all these deaths. What's this put you up to, eight? Or are there more nobody knows about?"

Sissy huffed, swallowing back tears threatening to rise. Crying might drown her in emotion that this man would surely see as guilt.

"Let's start at the beginning and we'll forget you being a bitch," the detective said, the word bitch riding extra emphasis.

"I'm tired. Are you charging me?" Sissy said.

"Damned right!" The detective flung his body forward and slammed his little hands on the steel table between them.

"But it's crazy. I didn't—"

The door opened again, and two familiar faces stepped inside. Both men. Both in fine blue suits. The one Sissy knew as Special Agent Lincoln Hunter cleared his throat. The one named Special Agent Jedidiah Waters said, "Detective Greenly, why did you instruct one of your men to erase more than six hundred hours of footage from Mr. John Nolan's surveillance cameras?"

The detective sneered. "'Cause it was all fake news. Hogwash and tall tales. Sasquatches, who'd ever believe it? Have to be plum stupid."

"Have to be plum short-sighted to think erasing evidence was a viable option to make a case stick to an innocent victim," Hunter said.

Sissy sighed and finally let the emotions show. This was an ordeal, and it was far from over, but it wasn't going to get drastically worse.

"How often do you do this?" Waters said. "Pin cases on victims."

The detective pushed to his feet. "This is my county and y'all aren't welcome."

"That's not how this works, little man. Come on, Sissy, let's take you someplace more hospitable," Hunter said.

Sissy pushed to her feet and became the meat of a special agent sandwich as she walked the short hall into the bullpen of cop desks—now mostly empty— and through the lobby. Outside, she followed to a black Dodge Charger and climbed in the back.

Waters sat shotgun and turned in his seat. "I have to ask: does it seem like sasquatches use telepathy? I mean, what are the chances you'd have to survive this kind of attack twice?"

"What do you mean?" Sissy said, though she got it because she'd wondered too.

Hunter got in and turned on the car. "He means, do

you think they target you?"

In the sanity and safety of the modern world, beneath modern lights, riding in a modern mode of transportation, she could only shake her head and laugh a single snort. "No. I needed money and found myself at Squacher-Con."

Hunter clucked his tongue against the inside of his cheek and pointed a finger gun at Sissy. "Ain't that always the way?"

Sissy began to sob.

Check out other great

Cryptid Novels!

Ian Faulkner

CRYPTID

Be careful what you look for. You might just find it.1996. A group of 14 students walked into the trackless virgin forests of Graham Island, British Columbia for a three-day hike. They were never seen again. 2019. An American TV crew retrace those students' steps to attempt to solve a 23-year-old mystery.A disparate collection of characters arrives on the island. But all is not as it seems. Two of them carry dark secrets. Terrible knowledge that will mean death for some – but a fighting chance of survival for others. In the hidden depths of the forests – man is on the menu. Some mysteries should remain unsolved...

Eric S. Brown

LOCH NESS HORROR

The Order of the Eternal Light, a secret organization have foretold the end of the human race. In order to save all humanity, agents of the Order must locate the Loch Ness Monster and obtain a sample of its blood for within in it is the key to stopping the apocalypse but finding the monster will be no easy task.

Check out other great
Cryptid Novels!

P.K. Hawkins

THE CRYPTID FILES

Fresh out of the academy with top marks, Agent Bradley Tennyson is expecting to have the pick of cases and investigations throughout the country. So he's shocked when instead he is assigned as the new partner to "The Crag," an agent well past his prime. He thinks the assignment is a punishment. It's anything but.Agent George Crag has been doing this job for far longer than most, and he knows what skeletons his bosses have in the closet and where the bodies are buried. He has pretty much free reign to pick his cases and he knows exactly which one he wants to use to break in his new young partner: the disappearance and murder of a couple of college kids in a remote mountain town.Tennyson doesn't realize it, but Crag is about to introduce him to a world he never believed existed: The Cryptid Files, a world of strange monsters roaming in the night. Because these murders have been going on for a long time, and evidence is mounting that the murderer may just in fact be the legendary Bigfoot.

Gerry Griffiths

DOWN FROM BEAST MOUNTAIN

A beast with a grudge has come down from the mountain to terrorize the townsfolk of Porterville. The once sleepy town is suddenly wide awake. Sheriff Abel McGuire and game warden Grant Tanner frantically investigate one brutal slaying after another as they follow the blood trail they hope will eventually lead to the monstrous killer. But they better hurry and stop the carnage before the census taker has to come out and change the population sign on the edge of town to ZERO.

Check out other great
Cryptid Novels!

Hunter Shea
THE DOVER DEMON

The Dover Demon is real...and it has returned. In 1977, Sam Brogna and his friends came upon a terrifying, alien creature on a deserted country road. What they witnessed was so bizarre, so chilling, they swore their silence. But their lives were changed forever. Decades later, the town of Dover has been hit by a massive blizzard. Sam's son, Nicky, is drawn to search for the infamous cryptid, only to disappear into the bowels of a secret underground lair. The Dover Demon is far deadlier than anyone could have believed. And there are many of them. Can Sam and his reunited friends rescue Nicky and battle a race of creatures so powerful, so sinister, that history itself has been shaped by their secretive presence? "THE DOVER DEMON is Shea's most delightful and insidiously terrifying monster yet." – Shotgun Logic Reviews "An excellent horror novel and a strong standout in the UFO and cryptid subgenres." –Hellnotes "Non-stop action awaits those brave enough to dive into the small town of Dover, and if you're lucky, you won't see the Demon himself!" – The Scary Reviews PRAISE FOR SWAMP MONSTER MASSACRE "B-horror movie fans rejoice, Hunter Shea is here to bring you the ultimate tale of terror!" – Horror Novel Reviews "A nonstop thrill ride! I couldn't put this book down." – Cedar Hollow Horror Reviews

Armand Rosamilia
THE BEAST

The end of summer, 1986. With only a few days left until the new school year, twins Jeremy and Jack Schaffer are on very different paths. Jeremy is the geek, playing Dungeons & Dragons with friends Kathleen and Randy, while Jack is the jock, getting into trouble with his buddies. And then everything changes when neighbor Mister Higgins is killed by a wild animal in his yard. Was it a bear? There's something big lurking in the woods behind their New Jersey home.Will the police be able to solve the murder before more Middletown residents are ripped apart?